I0582455

PRAISE FOR *SKELETAL LIGHTS FROM AFAR*

"Dear Reader, you will never have read anything quite like the luminous *Skeletal Lights from Afar*, I can promise you that. A master of voice, Roth's words become a ghost voice implanted in your psyche which remains long after you reach the end, offering you birds and flesh and bone. Indeed, they offer you the cycle of life, children climbing into bed between their parents to reclaim that shining moment of safety that is so fleeting to the last breath that awaits us all."

—Myfanwy Collins, author of *I Am Holding Your Hand*

"Reading this new book by Forrest Roth, I kept thinking, 'Here is an original voice.' Not exactly microfictions or prose poems, they blur those distinctions with meditation and observation and intellect, yet retain movement enough to sustain the tension of story. Forrest Roth has produced an accessible, yet challenging collection that will find an audience."

—Gary Fincke, author of *The Corridors of Longing*

WHAT BOOKS PRESS

AN IMPRINT OF

THE GLASS TABLE

COLLECTIVE

LOS ANGELES

ALSO BY FORREST ROTH

Line and Pause
The Sullen Pages (chapbook)
Gary Oldman Is A Building You Must Walk Through

SKELETAL LIGHTS
FROM AFAR

SKELETAL LIGHTS
FROM AFAR

FORREST ROTH

LOS ANGELES

Copyright © 2022 by Forrest Roth. All rights reserved.
Published in the United States by What Books Press,
the imprint of the Glass Table Collective, Los Angeles.

Library of Congress Cataloging-in-Publication Data

Names: Roth, Forrest, author.
Title: Skeletal lights from afar / Forrest Roth.
Description: Los Angeles : What Books Press, [2022] | Summary: "Collecting
    previously published flash fiction and prose poems, Skeletal Lights from
    Afar presents six galleries of enigmatic humans drifting towards
    destinations accidental and unknown"-- Provided by publisher.
Identifiers: LCCN 2022021580 | ISBN 9781733378901 (trade paperback)
Subjects: LCGFT: Flash fiction. | Prose poems.
Classification: LCC PS3618.O8578 S58 2022 | DDC 818/.6--dc23
LC record available at https://lccn.loc.gov/2022021580

Cover art: Gronk, *Untitled*, mixed media on paper, 2021
Book design by Ash Good, www.ashgood.com

What Books Press
363 South Topanga Canyon Boulevard
Topanga, CA 90290

WHATBOOKSPRESS.COM

CONTENTS

AUTUMNALS

RESIDUALS

NATURALS

FUNNY LITTLE BIRD

INADVERTENT PREY: they could be finches or robins or sparrows or nondescript, but never just themselves; they appear white-brown or red-brown or brown-brown or black-brown-white with a dull plume; they function less adequately than wind-up toys that break when stepped on because you can't see how cheap they are; they have no skill for scent, no taste for wind; they never travel anywhere warm, never drink water not spiked with their own shit or the shit of others; they never copulate when someone else is watching, but in secret, poorly kept, like a magician turning one tiger into two behind a sequined screen; they get sucked into the radiators of pick-up trucks while flying low; they hardly have any meat on their frames when you poke at them with a branch; they possess a heart that can fit in a locket that can be saved in a jewelry box that can be thrown in a backyard ditch; they have macaroni for bones; they fetch nothing on the black market, then become contraband *gratis* for those who swap clandestine sketchbooks just for edification on forbidden subjects.

This particular study reminds him of how I am when my neck is turned awkwardly as something catches my attention from behind for the last time, and is useful.

CLEAN DEAD LEAVES

WE CLEAN THE DEAD leaves because dead leaves do not clean themselves. Leaves, upon becoming dead, have only us to clean them; and when we are dead, we must leave to clean elsewhere. In the meantime, these leaves stay dead while we clean them, though dead leaves do not become clean leaves until we finish our cleaning.

Leaves made both clean and dead are of great consequence: dead leaves mean we are unclean, clean leaves mean we are not dead. We must have clean dead leaves, yet we cannot leave until our dead have been cleaned as well. The cleaned dead leave nothing but dead leaves, and they will remain dead should we leave cleaned leaves. So we must leave or clean the dead ourselves, and our dead, now cleaned, leave us to clean these dead leaves on our own. Will the dead never leave without being cleaned otherwise?

Let us clean them, leave, and be dead ourselves, as the leaves can clean us.

There are no leaves that are both clean and dead, however, once our dead leave for good. Under the leaves, our dead clean leaves for no one but the other dead. Please do not leave the dead clean before the leaves, then. The dead have failed to leave us clean.

FANTASY OF TREES IN SILVER

after Ingmar Bergman

LESSER WORLDS THIEVE, imprison a larger scale, they are
instructed before the scene borrowed from their uncle's *Fantasy of
Trees in Gold*, a subtle pagan theme from his native hinterlands almost
forgotten. His diminutive self preserves no austerity, either—slack
old amoralist, oddfellow at best guess—among the town's socialites
ghosting this rare performance. They have purified their skeletons
flagrante delicto, lit candles at vespers crying for their own syncopation.
Public festoons smell faintly of urine to the children as well. Camphor
vapors in their room on the second floor will be released later, then,
the dressers, bedposts already shellacked in hypnotist red, preventing
any motley of pillow feathers sticking to them, unlike their maid's
secret kisses. "You are always my empress," she teases the nephew and
his sluggish lapel while intrusive shadows outside appraise the lamps.
Snow illumes half a lifetime. Adrift, an adulterous wife tosses her
husband's armor away on a street corner; the lothario nudges it with
his greedy moccasin, inquires by aside if its owner has indeed perished.
Few corpses find themselves silent. To ignore the staircase set that had
been designed in a dream interrupted by an overly amorous couple,
the audience must abbreviate their murmuring in short spasms. They
call out the flame's knock on the convent latch with voices guttural
and rusty from misuse. A fine pastiche is ruined. But the children
hold their breath. They hope their uncle's inner turmoil ascends as

an archangel instead. Curtains, several curtains. In arrival of its bane, mature speaking is decreed unsavory in the private study by a scarab beetle collection crystal-encased above the letter table, icons of Holy Mother with Child in degraded orbit, and phases of the Arctic Circle expanding. This myriad reflects in the dome of a coffee spoon, which the children are pressed to follow as their surrogate father. The floor, however, is what they mostly consult. Set upon carpets diamonded indigo against lapis lazuli, the trim a macabre whitish hue christened *whalespackle*, the nephew plants himself to play war, deciding his marble chess pieces have ignored the lack of a Cartesian grid. He observes in detail angled visages, poor suitors for an iron helmet, their kneecaps built like anvils—yet the hoary battalion succeeds!—until each pawn seems to trade its weapon for a willow branch. Perhaps he is mistaken (the carver's renderings do lumber clumsy, imprecise). Conversions have been forbidden indoors for several decades. An infernal miracle? How the uncle, greatest Cataloguer to inhabit the Grand Arboretum, chooses overlooking this defies the innocent appeals of the nephew. "There," he points hurriedly to the disheveled greybeard, "and these aments . . ." a species which name fails in Latin since it slights a most favored paramour, she who had kept herself alive only to count alongside the uncle the Pyrrhic falling of heavy limbs. On frost-laden veil, torn, a riot of distant echoes bound somewhere wintry for his premature lambskin sect, a parlor mazurka as evensong.

PARCEL POST BELGIQUE

DANSVOORT POSTAL OFFICE

Rummaging through the stamp-drawer, I rarely drive myself from
deep rest so eager as to deliver something of such minimal value that
even a trainee could tell it misses the point of transatlantic service
of the Aeropostale. Avian species indeed! Yet what am I to do? It
does not involve a comrade. With noticeable disinterest Bruchet had
insisted, "Take this dredge away from me," and the acting postmaster
does what he is told without inquiring of its contents or of the
philosophies of his estranged Felice, whom I have never met beyond
Bruchet's crude estimations while milling about in his woodshop. All
the same, I will be adjusting myself to those imagined dimensions
and more approximately two-to-three weeks from tomorrow, giving
his letter due courtesy that professionalism can dictate, though this
customer lets me apply postage from my own wages. Business has
been bad, he insists. I cannot complain for spite's sake. Choosing
stamps provides a brief pleasure for me in this town anyway (Bruchet
can be a bit miserable to drink with, his nose a faucet to match his
mouth). Thus I cut and affix, my precious little winged ones, the
truest of your altruisms for her starving intuition, which, I am told
by him, is not so learned as to avoid your naturalistic meanderings
picture by picture in a thumbnail's glance—or so I dearly hope.

KAUW / CHOUCAS DES TOURS (0,23)

First to be called upon when needed, you prefer avoiding civil service while stenography lessons are on-going, though your struggling finances need these limited engagements. Besides, what is agreeable to you depends on the acute rationalization of present circumstance, leaving your distressed family to wonder if they will ever hear from you again. The land passing underneath takes on many splendid shapes that you could never realize back home. Up here, it seems all the tiny green dominoes are in play, assuming anyone below you understands the rules and does not notice that they are too far behind in the score to win back their losses. So your triumph is complete. Climb higher and you may yet understand the colonial designs that came to naught like museum pieces spirited away in the dead of night by underpaid security guards. In this sense, it remains difficult comprehending who dictates those lofty rationales you have always been suspicious of, if not that ingenious Dostoevskian landlady who uses passages from the New Testament to justify raising your rent. You start thinking this life could use another cruel tyrant; nonetheless, sacrifices entail that responsibility to others you have heard much about as of late. On the other hand, the Dhammapada says "Better to walk alone than keep the company of fools," or something to that isolating effect. You let this ancient wisdom console your mercilessly tortured soul up until you smell your dinner burning on the kitchen stove.

———

CIRLGORS / BRUANT ZIZI (0,05)

Stubborn to forget Versailles, as well as encyclopedic to a terminal degree, you are somewhat memorialized in an obscure piano solo attempted by music students who cannot move past their inflated sense of a Satie melody. During afternoons, your unintentional Cubist sketches of the public-at-large in charcoal have several distinct fascinations for amorous carriage-dwellers, gendarmes wandering their beat, and impolite couples at Père Lachaise further defacing Oscar Wilde's grave. Aroma therapy is undertaken when surveying the rose

bushes, except individuals of your species may not avoid old man
benches at certain hours of the day. Best tree branches claimed before
and after lunch. You say surprisingly few compliments in dislocation
and consider grimacing a primal insult. Keep your personality suited
to a business air about it, refuse to recognize your grandchildren no
matter how much they cajole for phony war stories. Speak beside the
point. Do not pursue the spontaneous marching band. There is enough
time for that, the song plays in your thoughts, when your drawings are
returned for a crumpled franc-note inside a Havana cigar box.

———

RUIGPOOTUIL / CHOUETTE DE TENGMALM (0,10)

My lord of goodnesses! You have turned out this evening to spread
around the roost, yet you arrive to find the quality cognacs untapped.
The host does not offer mice, even when asked politely for them, lost in
the sonic of an interior haze he creates by bi-partisan committee like his
own well-planned sarcophagus since he has dispatched social duties to
his boorish wife. Unfortunately, you miss anticipating the awkward faux
pas and spill the cheapest drinks on her. Blame a lush, madcap desire for
the smaller she-fowls invited—also your distraction by the urgency of
their breasts. A mortal fear of them and apricot liqueur sends you to the
walk-in closet to examine the pelts hanging like trophies, guessing which
belong to the sophists and which belong to the greedy philanthropists.
You return in a better mood, but the parlor game you have devised is a
dismal failure. The guests prefer leaving at the first sight of sunrise you
abhor just to show who they plan to vote for in the run-off election.

———

KWARTELKONIG / RÂLE DE GENÊTS (0,30)

You, there—do you not think one is prettier to be of this world rather
than in it? What price affords the simple comfort of being? Can your life
transcend a mere cautionary tale reinvented for our eternal entertainment?
Alas, would you have the privacy to consider these meaningless questions

forwarded to your secretary after a brief incarceration. All your steps so
carefully choreographed, your bemused and indifferent lovers scheduled
day by day so they never cross paths with each other—even if they
are easily deceived—not to mention an elaborate doppelgänger your
stepmother trains as a red herring, right down to the funny squeak in your
crescendoes, the trademark signature a glorious empire of the senses has
been built upon; yes, a wonder that a single hour may pass uneventful,
without the fateful gaze of clamor stealing your finest performance to date.

———

TAPUIT / TRAQUET MOTTEUX (1,00)

Shaker of the rocks, quick as the sharpest promontory suicides
cast themselves from. On the coast during April, you are known
to disparage handkerchief-waving and other devout signs of humility.
Should you see these events happen below, you strike back as though
challenged in a forum for aspiring gentlemen. Taking cue from outdoor
artists working on their living room canvases, you come to view your ugly
self in a colorful contradiction of nursery blue and funnel-cake yellow, in
addition to a dim throat-blush that hinders your chances during mating
season. Second-hand suits assist your dapper attire as you point your beak
towards the overworked letter-carrier and his plus-stuffed bin on creaky
plastic wheels. These premeditated attacks force you to repair to a tavern,
drink heavily on purpose so you may dispense poor advice to hapless
tourists regarding train routes from the city. The premier hotel you
frequent gives no discounts for celebrity. Only the attaché, despite having
never read a single page of Proust, understands where your seething really
comes from, and he offers keeping it secret for a generous stock tip.

———

TORENVALK / FAUCON CRECERELLE (0,75)

Decorum suggests there is nothing as invigorating as the sight of
majesty in miniature form, which makes you wonder where the
snickering is coming from as you walk into the ballroom. There is an

additional cringing sensation felt from having to hear Tchaikovsky for
the umpteenth time this month while St. Petersburg keeps stealing the
headlines. Scanning the crowd, everyone faintly resembles that clumsy
inspector you caught hanging from your antique rod-iron trellis. But
you must admit to yourself that the glowing, celestial décor is the very
fishbowl of your previously untrammeled existence, and the company not
so disagreeable that you could swim about it happily until your forehead
gets sore from hitting the glass all the time. If only the scandalous widow
from Brussels had not shown up here! Seeing her again reminds you
of that countryside tryst in a garden maze. Then your luck truly sours
when a well-meaning yet clueless friend you go grouse hunting with
introduces you to her, and you both must feign ignorance of each other
for the remainder of the evening lest her children's lawyers catch on. Your
final waltz together is particularly brutal, her complaining about the
impracticality of political dissent being the surest sign of the proletariat's
inherent weaknesses for engaging fundamental social reform, while you
rebut that the snails could have stood more garlic butter.

———

WINTERTALING / SARCELLE D'HIVER (0,05)

Modest to your own infuriation, you travel short distances and are
repeatedly found by some snowy brook that shares other seasons not so
romantic. A flair for punctuality follows your dramatic telegraphs asking
to be read aloud or passed around in groups at café demonstrations
which break up premature. "Unless you care to understand what grand
cause I have taken up out here," you choose to address the audience in
absentia, "do not bother writing me back—for I will be dead to you all."
To which they agree because you are hardly the Master of Guilt.

———

GEOORDE FUUT / GRÈBE À COU NOIR (0,23)

It is quite well you should descend and rest for a moment since you
are nearing the terminus, meaning the conclusion of official duties

that were not so extensive to begin with, that is, other than what a near-sighted clerk at the Amsterdam bureau deems as correct postage, but here is your noble reward for contemplating the notion, dubious at it may appear to someone of your impeccable breeding, of the philatelic infallibility of Nederlanders: a long, well-deserved green settee to platter your crimson stare for the coming night's festivities before a lit fireplace adorned with bitter holiday berries and nightshade, you waiting for your forearms to find precious companionship outside these tempered words.

————

SOMEWHERE OVER COPENHAGEN (PERHAPS)

I remember Bruchet laughing at me one night at the tavern, well into a third round of ales, calling me a tedious sot when I confessed to him that postal delivery lets me live without any God, and this bears resemblance to plaintive faith every religion must start with, I believe. Who knows when, where, how? What can be proven if indeed successful? I toss the dice until my best intentions are met, but often I am never certain of what I really do. For whom is so consistent in both action and thought? Since it has been explained to me the environment becomes at this time of year icy and inhospitable where Felice resides, alone in a ramshackle abode hidden by conifers my mind's eye creates for her, I cannot guess whether she will be alive when your flock arrives to spread my humble message. Hopefully you will temper Bruchet's vitriol in the envelope, its edges slathered by his roguish tonguebuds unforgiving. It remains terrible for me to consider I am responsible for its contents being sent. If nothing else, I do possess an address where he has left her to collect the mail. Having thrown you to the winds in this matter, thank you for your charity and determination. Sincerely. The acting postmaster's blessings in a smudgy purple ink ascribes unworthy your soon-to-be frozen countenances: when traveling anywhere with the proper currency, does your will not stand up to the distance? All I can say is, be the kindest sortings should you arrive local. Remind her she may draw warmth from below as well as above.

TENDER SPOILS

FOR MANY HOLIDAY SEASONS, at a few three-star coastal
resorts, his services temporarily retained themselves. The modest title he
took turned upon subtle charity: Head of Outdoor Decorative Fruits.
Management made plastic coverings optional. He fixed his preparations
at low tide. Pitted cherries hollow-clean, orange rinds devising
aerodynamic, banana diagonals. Then these portions for the guests rolled
up and over in a generous, awkward pile. In thickening heat the breakfast
grew less savory. A fragrant decay. They told him it was unmistakable.

Semi-retirement seemed a welcome imperative. He had shared
a place within another place up against the surf. Cheap rent. His
apologies had no effect on her. She wavered beside his bed. She missed
the fiercest suns. "For chrissakes," she scolded, "strawberries can't always
be symmetrical." So when she slept he left early to harmonize the
deck chairs. Before dawn hesitating pairs—and not necessarily proud
couples—walked the shoreline. They were talking, but they could have
been friendlier, he thought. They could let him eavesdrop for a change.

He stayed there on the patio. Those conversations did look
blameless at sunrise. Picture perfect. He stopped making himself upset.
Leaning in, he started assembling pineapple rings as bottle flies huddled
on the platter nearby. They were an altogether convincing devotion.

KEEPING WITH

BETTER AWAKENED than awake, rare grey eyes satisfied stay on the path in a public city park. A non-color better than bringing color film. *Forget the bird*, she thinks, *take note.*

Trained by consecutive male subjects of the camera's gaze, he is in her keeping. Having snapped another private *him* by accident for the closet collection while searching for the falcon nesting in a high-rise condo, her camera points down in rest while the municipal rifle she follows remains up. Many in anonymity never find themselves under glass. But she leaves this impromptu portrait unframed, tucked under a fraying sweater seldom worn.

She calls *him* what he names himself to her later.

————

From artistic statement (discarded)—
What accrues in a background transfers itself to the unconscious. Wet sediment gives way, collapses, settles, rests. Then a pattern resists being found. Nature defies.

————

At this recent subject's discretion, a Turkish talisman arrives by mail for her. With his compliments: the piercing, glazed ocular of blue. A touch of menace. Will she think some part of the world is here, or does she even have to try? She makes a necklace of it. She doesn't make it. She suffers a stretch of bad publicity—all because of the bird—her full name spelled out phonetically by imperative, or spelled wrong altogether, no one says it right, no one thinks it's right, and he doesn't think it's right, it's not a name under a photo to begin her with. It shouldn't be her peregrine falcon killed in mid-frame. He insists she had promised everyone who promised to crowd her at the gallery.

Meal elsewhere. Try discussing. Consider the poor poor bird's plume ripped apart. Consider the not-so-errant bullet. Not hers. Camera shot holds together. Hers. They try. They hold.

———

From artistic statement (retained)—

Chance does not revive bone with the flesh. Photography does not. A failing of avian species is their devoutness, which we pay no attention.

———

She refuses to believe anything all over again.

Newer duties take up her confusion. It may also include her hiding fabric softener in the darkroom, scenting their laundry with his car keys—provided the latest *him* stored away passes through her closet undetected. She feels confident. Winter never arrives.

For a while, being recognized outside entails wearing her evil eye.

GLOSSIES

SHE RECALLS self-portraiture, signing the table's underside in
black crayon as a child with another, lovelorn regret. These are hidden
consequences prior to hired help levitating her body while they titter
in outlandish brogues, admire how accessible the refectory shower is.
Without her train, her silken whiteness clings about too tight, shapes
her firm aureoles to pucker at attention. We are staring, serious. Certain
queasy heaves rush one youth holding his divan pillow, who motions
to an ice water pail the matron is preparing and dunks his head. We
hear molars crunch wood chips (a libidinal control the priest had
distributed). Rose petals spill out of his pockets.

Exactly how does a pond make us tranquil—unless preservatives
in the marigold arrangement will steel a guest or three? But they are
already an incoherent mumble about histories of thrilling arrivals in
oft-anointed tongues. It orchestrates their well-behaved stupor, these
sniffles and snucks which reach deafening crescendos, unaware she is
sunlit, propping her raccoon eyes against the gazebo in full bloom.

With her deepest blessings we should stay plain for a few hours more.
On the mountainside awaits a reception housing red roast beef in the prime
of its life, swimming in silvery *au jus* which mirrors additional trappings.

OCCASIONAL

OUT OF THE WAY, the storm chasers had fled towards the danger, only returning at dusk, but still hungry. We had a few eggs left which hadn't flown away, a loaf of bread not broken. "We'll eat it all," they boasted, and we believed them until they did eat it all. Then they noticed we had nothing left and asked if they could have that as well. We gave them the last of it for their equipment to record. They laughed, patted each other on the back. "The best yet!" they cheered, watching the dials move, the needles tremble. Our admiration was a helpless thing, far less than what the weather can be on occasion here, yet we waved to the gathering crowd.

THE BEAR PLANET EDICT

TO CANCEL the negative fortune of Mercury's unexpected declination, the Mayor of our town issued an Inauspicious Event Edict: *All households must abscond with their youngest male child to the wilderness.* Sent away, our youngest brother grew to be a wildman—albeit discontentedly so, for his life's aspiration was to build with concrete and glass, to design the crystal towers of the future. He took his revenge by sneaking back into our home one night, inking sepia circles on our heads with porcupine quills while we slept. Thus began a difficult chapter for my family. The last marked family had been bulldozed in their home after a Public Cleansing Edict, yet we managed postponing this fate thanks to our father's personal connection to the Mayor's astrologist-medium. The outer rim planets, she informed us, had aligned in an irregular orbit around their new fixed locus at the bottom of our valley. In response the currents of the streams had backed up into a tributary where opportunistic bears were now depositing their excrement. We were stuck, then, with both permanent forehead markings and a wafting stench, though both tribulations were to be overcome in tandem, the astrologist-medium divined upon sizing up my older sister. In the meantime, our brother mocked us with bitter glee. He danced outside, grimaced while forming a circle with his hands, and flaunted his puny genitals. My parents resigned themselves; my sister refused. She salted our entire front lawn, thus burning the bottom of her wayward brother's soles since they were cracked with chilblains and infected with ringworm from the bear tributary he had been frequenting. We assumed this was where he limped off to cool his heels. My sister was not convinced. She and I pursued him, taking a shovel with us, to see if some salve was buried underneath his lair that could rid the markings. Tucked away in the farthest corner of the terrible woods, a mud-packed hut greeted us (our brother was an architect after all!), with a singular hazy yellow glow creeping from its portal. Our brother, it seemed, had no skill with fire: he simply tended to a blazing stack of pine branches while the sores on his feet singed and smoked. My sister had seen enough. Grabbing the shovel from my hand she barged in and drove the sharp edge into the side of his head. A thick, reddish fluid flowed from the gaping wound onto the dirt floor. She stirred the pooling membranes with her finger, tracing the circle on her head and mine with nascent remorse; and slowly, the markings faded away. We were powerless, however, to stop the bears discovering the putrefying scent of our brother. They eventually disposed of his body in their natural appetites, but not before we entered their den to give our proclamation regarding what physical form he would soon become. In front of them, under the thrall of my sister's feral stare, I shook our bloodied shovel while imagining it was the axis on which their whole world must revolve.

A FEW AREAS OF NOTE
AT PROSPECT PARK

MIDWOOD TRAIL

Two things indicated on the posted Visitor's Guide Map at the park entrance never to be encountered by first-time hikers along this popular trail: the cartoon-like mystery of the giant White-Out exclamation point, and soothing splotches of mismatched tertiary colors. Various cigarette burns on the map, however, may correctly show potential areas of unprovoked moose attacks and / or used beer can pipes with salvageable resin.

———

SULLIVAN HILL

Named for the second explorer of the region who accidentally passed through in 1697 while trapping squirrels. The original explorer's name was also Sullivan, not related; he arrived three years earlier, was a clever frontiersman, and wiped out a small Native village nearby in a drunken rage. The second Sullivan, by all written accounts, never touched a drop in his life nor did he consummate his only marriage. Intense scholarly and public debate continues today regarding the historical legacy of both men.

———

RAVINE

This has no name. Park Management looking into the matter.

————

PROSPECT VALLEY STATE PARK ZOO

New visitors are often entertained by how the large green algae spot on "Nanny" the polar bear's backside sometimes resembles the Virgin Mary puckering her lips.

————

CHILDREN'S CORNER

Despite the misnomer, parents have the Park Management's assurance that their children do not own anything here, thus all parties can escape easily.

————

FUNTIME WONDERLAND CAROUSEL OF JOY

Dismantled and removed in July 2011 due to a fatal unicorn accident, this despite large, organized parent protests after public announcement of Park Management decision. Temporary interfaith memorial erected on site by the deceased's family removed by legal injunction sought from the National Atheists Coalition. Plans to pave and convert into a parking area for the Children's Corner have been put on hold due to massive state budget cuts. The plot is currently sitting vacant. It is not scheduled to be mowed anytime soon.

BEETS

BEETS ARE EASIEST, but he brings them home anyway. Needs them for their hearts, for the working parts other vegetables do not have. He slices and cooks them all—only at night, so the neighbors can sleep through it—and lets those sticky stains fill him up to the morning bedsheets. Later, everyone who is invited for dinner sees the passion of his effort. A more private record exists, too, of containment and measurements; however, he is sure he will lose it at some point. If he has not already. Beets take up enough space in his memory as it is. All they have is each other there. He considers a new cutting board as well, cleaning the trails on the linoleum, those gruesome little footsteps dragging themselves. Yet he decides not. The neighbors will get suspicious should they look through his window and find him with no beets and no stains, he fears. He knows they will offer theirs for him to visit next door, to come inside and cook, tell him offhand their daughter has recently divorced, though is looking again.

CURIO

THE LOVED ONES come beached Smooth Sphere Warm mostly.
Crags finger possibilities abandoned: mere sandspots taken home.
Polished by Clean Preservation Shine. Assigned an Importance Place
Position. They will sit Big Buddha Heavy (not Amida Sad Skinny) with
Gravity Purpose Volume. Next to the Faulkner Steinbeck Whitmans.
Or next to the Kafka Proust Shakespeares instead. But rare crusts do
not beach well. Why does wandering permit itself, except when Cold
Jagged Rough? Those are left collected undertide. They will learn at
Briny Deep Ominous, on a shelf where the Mishima Plath Woolfs lost
their spine to flood.

JOVIALS

DRIFT

ON OR BEFORE A FLAT, the horizon had summoned sleek Opportunity to take any bus being maintained before Greyhound in Cincinnati gives through and up. "Just when Ohio gets their fleetworthy shit together since," she extends, unbuttons herself aislewise from memory alone of those ridings.

In retrospect, it is parental-like advice offered about shaving with cold water that turns germane in a few on-board shudders. Minus your travel kit stuffed with miniature oatmeal soap, hotel toothbrushes shrink-wrapped, she opens something else of hers. The niceties she has does for, then what luxury hits grooved pavement while locked inside a would-be water closet, dropping her least favorite aunt's compact down the blue chute, cabin lights fading out muddy, yet strop-sharp? *This land is our window for territory*, some tender brochure goes on. Red-eyes cramped may come in handy for the unscheduled pull-over when, in the next seat, she refuses getting up a smile at coach fare.

To more immediate mind: advancement—north or south—towards spending a lifetime from the nearest authority.

"As rivers loom in sight," she whispers, "they beckon in sleep—"

Almost she finishes: "—though drivers don't take a piss slumped over the steering wheel so normal."

BUSINESS

WHEN THE SPRING RAINS come, all the market street proprietors must bring in their mannequins, or risk them being washed away in the resulting floods. I have lost a few myself this way and, considering they are not cheap to come by, I have learned to rue the disappearance of each one more than anyone else in this coastal province who didn't stay inside: a grandparent here, a six-year-old there, what does it matter. They tell us during the funerals that it does. By that time, when the clouds have passed, I've spent most of the week searching for my lost mannequin and finding instead distant relations still alive who I had thought been swept away during the previous flood, or another hapless bystander who went out photographing the downpour, now floating silent in a stream. This inevitability is saddening, yet few things can be dressed up as a mannequin suitable for a drowned town. I've tried broomsticks potted in pails of hard cement, dressed up to no avail. One of those distant relations I discovered worked well, even a hapless bystander or two—until someone reported me for that. These perfectly good mannequins laying around, waiting to help me out. If only it didn't rain so much. Then people in this godforsaken tourist trap would mind their own business.

TRADE

BROUGHT MISS the last of the girls and it was time to settle. "More's the pity," she objected, a few crocodile tears diving into and out of her change purse.

From these modest earnings I purchased, among other filterables, some black tea in bulk that might fit square into a Korean hatchback. It was then I noticed scratches from their painted fingernails against the back window. Guess I had stopped listening to them since San Simeon: the hotel water shortage put me in a bad mood while I showered. An ocean begging right out in front.

Miss could pick these places blindfolded. The view tried importing from Greek seas, supposedly copying Hellenic cliffs, or so the receptionist wanted to sell me. Her office had iffy wallpaper. Running squirrels. Not much safer in our double room. The girls had gone ahead and already pinned their faces to the pillows. Judging by the activity on our balcony, the town was getting touristy that night. I opted us to stay in. The girls suggested holding a séance for the dinner we were supposed to have and drew the blinds. Ghostly knives and forks and plates arrived, they claimed in the dark. Maybe I saw a spoon, but that was it. Switching the lights back on, this fresh blue-haired one said I looked irate enough to start breaking legs. I camped outside in my Daiyoon just in case.

Next morning, they were snug-tight, sleeping in the same bed without a care. My neck was cramping. "Let's go," I chop-chopped at them, "she's waiting and I'm hungry." While dressing they asked me to buy them stamps. For postcards later. As instructed, I didn't promise anything. They got their boots laced up and marched hardly moving, as if they liked stepping on their own toes. Out the door slow they went. Quiet. Single file down the stairs. I sat on the corner of their bed. Mine was still made.

"Always happy as horny clams in the end," Miss reminded me. She asked if I'd care to travel.

I decided, after a big lunch, that the passenger windows didn't need cleaning.

Took a few miles for going solo to sink in. Almost screwed myself over in Reno. Then I watched a fine smash at an intersection there. Oil and antifreeze spattered every which way. The light changed when I felt lucky for ignoring the excitement, smelling that tea hiding in the dashboard. I also felt warm. Figured it was me heading all Alabama from there on.

Thought I'd drive right by, no rubbernecking.

Didn't want any trouble keeping my posture up.

THE WIN

I LOST IT ALL at Eldergarden, including my last two $100 chips paired up on the table like my paltry manhood in her clutch. Have rolled, been rolled. Thought I could admire her for that. Until I couldn't. Card after card drawn, she kept beating the house, yours truly. Added to my suffering, her aimless yarns about Atlantic City, some place along the Louisiana bayou Interstate called L'Auberge she never pronounced right, the Biggest Little City in our state—"You know," she sighed fondly, "the town with the juiciest double bacon cheeseburgers." Those classy joints. Pulling her highchair closer to the table, she smiled as if remembering who I was. "Come to think of it, I learned tricks from a dealer as young as you," she said while laying down her cards in a rush, maybe realizing from the wall clock that *The Wheel of Fortune* was starting, "and you're a much better loser than he was." That sealed it. With one finger she pushed a $10 chip back to me, for my last supper. The others she scooped up, admired, and put in her plastic tumbler as she slow motioned off the chair to join her friends. Behind me the room already gathered its excitement since the returning champion on *The Wheel* was a retiree, "with sixteen grandchildren to round up and smooch later," according to his bio. The chants went up, "Trip to Venice!", "Knew you'd hit Bankrupt!", "Don't buy a goddamn vowel!" Quietly I put my cards away. I keep the curse to myself. So easy for her to be swayed by the mere material, ditching my tiny Mecca in green felt for the adult's glorified Spelling Bee. But I left my mark. The victorious word of victory itself was already planted on her ancient lips: the name of a seventeenth grandchild yet to be born, the name of that someone who will flee in a violent rainstorm with the last hundred and twenty-four dollars left in the United States of Winning.

WHO DOESN'T ENJOY A GOOD SAUSAGE

BECAUSE CONFESSIONS are the worst possible vehicle for sincerity: I haven't been the only proprietor of the Red Crest Pet Shop to pass off expired merchandise to Farmer Jed's Meat Market next door. In fact, as I've been told by my wife's grandmother, a clandestine arrangement has been enforced between the Pet Shop and Farmer Jed himself since Red Crest's incorporation in the 1940's, mostly in the form of Jed sending business back to us. Seniors stocking up on ground chuck who miss the presence of a cocker spaniel, curious foodie hipsters buying python meat looking for live exotics, those sorts. A strange correlation exists between them that people who never run a pet shop aren't aware of, these devoted carnivores needing animal company after stocking up their freezers. "You'll see what I mean," Jed told me as he picked up some gerbils laid low by a malfunctioning A/C unit one night out back. And I did. Can't say I felt good about it. The whole arrangement does have a certain sense which unnerves me. Maybe because Jed's customers know what they're buying. Or none of it makes any difference—"We're better off that it came from next door instead of Argentina," I can hear the content folk of Red Crest profess. I'm not speaking any revelations here. That's what prevents my sleeping recently. "What good's owning up to it," I complain to my wife, "when no one in town cares one way or the other?" Feeding our lone Asian carp in a tank meant for smaller species, she shrugs at my dismay. She thinks this fish'll grow large enough someday to set it free in the river nearby. I doubt it has any conception of the outside, a land where there are honest people lurking about, but I don't tell her nothing as she watches the carp endlessly bump its nose against the glass.

SHORT TIME WITH HULA GIRL

DASHBOARD JESUS having flown out the hard way through my windshield, Hula Girl moves in on his turf. I spent nearly three months in traction mulling over how I hadn't managed to follow his way, my best charm against dumb accidents. So it happens. Across this world a little plastic Jesus sits on every other dashboard, and most of them go bust eventually. Realizing that was more painful than this shaft they put in my leg, or the Dear John letter I got while sedated.

If I had wanted only a token decoration, I would've stuck Hula Girl up there in my view of the road and been done with it. In advance of happier memories, then, that's what I do when I get my new wheels. No one's ever that healthy (or patient) after a hospital discharge.

I remember someone I was seeing before our graduation buying her, this during our trip to Honolulu as a reward, what had been strictly a gag gift to toss in a box later. Fun times while they lasted. Honestly, however, I was more serious about Dashboard Jesus. Hula Girl was a passing fancy. Dashboard Jesus could've also had such appeal, I wanted to convince myself—I just needed to think about it long enough. And he did, but only after the big break-up, so to speak. Very inconvenient timing on his part. Like I should talk, though.

Yeah yeah, I totally get how Hula Girl's supposed to be an unconscious substitute for her, the one from Hawaii who should still be hanging around. But, whatever. Neither of them can be a true stand-in for Dashboard Jesus, his own sexy hips, his mirthless smile, his unspoken promises while I speed along. Despite my various betrayals, I try remaining upbeat while looking at her. I start feeling like someone else may yet care for me, except a shooting pain up my leg as I force the clutch, a vague forsaking of what I missed from afar: a turn, a warning, a warm breeze passing through and finding my welcoming face.

SOME BASEBALL STORIES

THIS WILL BE A STORY about baseball which must take its cue
from other stories about baseball. A game of men and weapons and
lines and empty spaces. It may be like the ancient boardgame Go,
assuming the cheering fans can think of the players as blank stones
upon which only allegiance is written, though forgetting at the same
time that baseball only has twenty-five men to a team. In this regard,
baseball somewhat resembles Go. Or could it resemble Go much more?
Is baseball not as original as the cheering fans believe? The first baseman
has to be crying about something out there— why can't it be that?
Nothing in baseball is sadder than a story where a player is distressed
because he realizes mid-game what an unoriginal sport baseball is,
recalling a deceased Japanese grandfather with whom he played Go and
always lost to because the old man was relentless, even with his own
grandchildren. No, that guy was a bastard, this first baseman recalls,
which is also a comparable trope to other baseball stories he knows.
Perhaps too many stories. There should be a story instead where the
shortstop makes a routine throw to first base but the first baseman
refuses to make the catch because he decides the lack of originality in
his life has become overwhelming. The idea of this story takes root:
allegiance cast aside, blank stone comes to life and renounces all forms
of bastardy, especially as it relates to allegorical warfare. His orbital
socket may need mending from this simple play he misses as the ball

hits his face, but hell that's all good. Won't take no marching orders from some lousy unoriginal story. Fans can go screw themselves, too, he decides while heading to the dugout as the boos and curses cascade down upon him. That goddamn net behind home plate isn't for anyone's protection, he tells his stunned coach on the way to the showers, it's another insult.

THE ALCOHOLIC'S RETURN

MY MISTAKE when they threw the alcoholic out. She wanted to help her. All that was left was to make the poor lush a ticker-tape parade. "We'll never get her back in," I protested. Working a fever-pitch at a napkin cluster under the table, and another, and another still, she had a fist-full of paper debris ready to celebrate her return. Had I held off my complaint to the manager, she'd be engaging us in some intellectual panhandling. But I glanced over at the bar. "Sorry about that," a bar girl apologized afterwards, bringing us two beers on the house, not expensive ones. I let her drink them both while she kept tearing napkins under the table, not letting me out of her sight. Oh, she'll come back, she insisted.

THE GOVERNOR SAYS

TOO YOUNG, too certain of my artificial control over anything, I had listened to a bored, wise-cracking Disney World tour guide inform us paying visitors that Cinderella Castle could be dismantled section by section within an hour and safely secured in the event of an imminent nuclear attack. I laughed at this because I didn't know if it was true. To this day I still don't know if it is true, but now I don't laugh when I think of it. I prefer keeping the guide's dubious initiative in a natural state of suspension. His claim, I try telling my wife to no avail, had taken the form of a most reassuring memory: the best of each and every one of us may yet be saved from the worst with a little effort from others, even if in piecemeal.

———

The governor, seated at a folding American Beer Pong Association table in his garage for his nightly live address, is most displeased with us bad citizens in these times of continual unprecedent. He knows 64% of our state's electorate impossibly lusts for the younger, more with-it governor in the neighboring state whose imaginative protocols make people there leap for joy. And these impossible lusts are having a detrimental effect upon the public health crisis, or, as he says with exasperation, "Look, I'm sorry, I've been in this pathogenic stew before, too, and man have I ever, but you all gotta get with the fucking program, okay?"

The fifth consecutive night we've been duly warned, my wife and I. We are to stay home clutching each other with second re-runs and low-budget telethons playing in the background until the next address. She weeps as usual, no doubt recalling former glory days advising him on the campaign trail before the big shake-up, and insists I listen carefully, so carefully to him. She turns up the volume. Over the dusty, off-tune notes of a frontier saloon piano in the corner he plays, I'm forced to hear the governor singing our state anthem with a peculiar skill, a halting reverence which, many years ago, had breathed to life an improbable landslide.

The following night his incumbent poise returns. He issues a stern correction after putting away his pocket comb. He tells us he didn't really use the word *fucking* the last time. Therefore, he is compelled to speak plain to us all from here on out. Because that was our own deviant minds at play.

———

From our tawdry siestas together, you know how I would operate instead in my glorious administration. Retrofitted mobile command platforms with hovercraft technology. Jetpack-wearing postal workers deploying large-scale airdrops of bundled mail into emptied swimming pools. Reduced-size supermarkets selling inventory sorted into three primary subsistence groups of Liquid, Processed Matter, and Vegetable Matter for more sanitary purchase through refurbished automat machines. University students safely attending classes through astral body projection with designated and trained pedagogical shamans. You nod with your eyes closed, tell me I would've been a great governor, maybe the greatest ever, and begin your drift into easier sleep next to me, curled up loose in the sheets. But my finest idea remains elusive. Entire urban and suburban neighborhoods re-zoned and reconstructed into ensconced labyrinthine structures to prevent residents from crossing paths with anyone they don't want to cross paths with, as well as finding their way back home if they stray too far. Yes, an ambitious policy. "Haven't worked out the details yet," I want to reveal while I can keep you awake.

———

It's our scheduled night for the roving CDC monitors. My wife watches the governor implore us again not to ruin ourselves, her hand on her chest. Irritated, she asks me if I've left our rec room beanbag in the driveway for them. "Is it Sweeps Week already," I mumble to myself outside, though not that I'd expect you to come here again. My head stays low as this oversized leather sphere I drop hits the concrete, deflating at first with a mushy whisper. The sound almost matches the false silence in our neighborhood, but no. A slow hissing which then starts suggests an audience paying closer attention to the heavily recycled plotlines this week.

AFTERBIRTHING

SHE AND I ARE a pre-determined number listing about only for the eventual reminders of our silliness: this exhibit space guarded by eight-foot-tall steel wool pads. Someone must have figured a dozen Lucite-encased vacuum cleaners won't return my attention, either. We both ball ourselves up together tight in boredom, waiting in line, prone to an insincere activity keeping me from saying to her, "Here we are again for the first time."

Yet reading palms, she contends, is a worthwhile diversion. Thankfully it could be her second or third favorite with me. Because the mystical braille prompts her denial of inauspicious fortunes for crosshatched ones such as mine, she feels my worse luck might be avoided if re-interpretation aligns itself with better luck (hers, I suppose). Except I had failed confessing, under any rain to date, that it only takes a mother, that a small, delicate knife inscribing the softening flesh upon my stepping out from her womb has conjured enough artificial destinies. Can I be forgiven for not mentioning it? Maternal talismans are awkward with no reliable *later* to address, with little alignment to gain.

For an old protective rage, I cannot be the merest hope of erstwhile men despite what is insisted by all the highly vulnerable in attendance.

Nonetheless, the bright light finds divination pleasing. She reads away. Maybe I let her go ahead as well. She seems to bargain on

moments remaining between us which clarify what future will occur—
since my *later* never arrives—though she misplaces her clairvoyance.
It will prove anything in the hushed shuffle before she and I enter a
grocery bag much larger than our own possible lives.

FAMILIALS

ECHO

I SAW MY SON last at, I think—Contemporary. A monstrous inflatable installation, which wasn't the fun diversion he thought it was. That was what had lured him. He ran ahead of me while I tiredly lingered near a statue, and soon he disappeared behind a wall, I suppose. All I could hear was his muffled laughing. Then I couldn't hear anything.

Alone in this wing, I asked a guard in the adjacent one if he had seen my son, about this tall, I motioned with my hand. "Please don't touch the paintings, ma'am," he replied, looking straight ahead. I asked a young couple on an audio tour, who peevishly lowered their audio-wands, shrugged, and continued looking at a smiling woman with neon-frame sunglasses, nodding their heads to what the audio-wands told them. I went back downstairs to consult a receptionist. Twenty-five dollars. Twenty for students and seniors.

I returned home for dinner. My husband seemed interested while we ate until he wasn't. "Can't be so bad," he determined before clearing the table, "those are some top-notch exhibits he can take in. Best schooling there is."

Turning off the bedside light, I couldn't disagree.

Especially when it rains, I like to visit the museum as often as I'm allowed. The paintings in the Contemporary wing are lovely in their own odd way, to be sure, but I prefer the Hellenic wing. Or East Asian.

Or maybe British. Someone else usually reminds me of my preference while I sit on one of the benches for a while, then I will move myself to another bench to find the quiet again. A voice can travel far along these marble hallways.

PROUST'S MOUSTACHE

My BROTHER AND I had often debated whether we could get our
father to shave his moustache off, to see if his literary sophistication
remained intact without it. A direct request when we were in private
school had failed miserably. Instead of studying *The Brothers Karamazov*
for a full term, we studied him. It was worth it. The second time
around, for Father's Day, we presented him a gold-plated razor
(functional but, undermining our intent, a novelty not meant to
be used), encased in a lined wooden box with an engraving on top:
Thanks For The Memories. We did better with this. He returned a
gracious laugh. "Would anyone have insinuated as politely to Proust?
Or Nietzsche?" Not Nietzsche, I thought. His vortex of facial hair can
hardly be considered a proper moustache—may as well come out and
say it to the guy. Proust, on the other hand? First-class work. A triumph
by his nurtured follicles. Always impeccably groomed in photos. And
I'm certain he would have been devastated had a friend handed him
a razor in mocking adoration. My brother probably had misgivings
along this line. He suggested the gift was a total bust afterwards, as our
father's moustache resolved to keep an imperious mien. He even dyed
it younger with a coloring kit. Compelled to salvage our gag later in
light of his renewed tenacity, I could only imagine for myself his clean-
shaven face, growing more and more thankful I never knew how many
of his mother's kisses died underneath that furry umbrella.

DRAWSTRING

A WORK WE SLEW this for: bringing it out of it, the little cotton-piece this bind—if he can watch us chore him afar and how there he is him. Big bright. Holy-rolly. Too crimson from cot to dry brook, yet we carry down where he has no sleep. Cranky with our touching. Cornmeal doesn't warm up, makes us tender to his slights. A good chance will change him worse instead of being raised in our apron. It needs whisking, we shout. It craves an egg! Slipperiest fish they all say. Morning starts to demand lots from us. He means pushing away to collect himself, we suppose. Thinking. Pointing over there, that far ground—that's maybe okay for a well. Must get digging through lean tight deep. Shame's in the needing is what he teaches. He shows us tugging any earth. Eats a mouthful. Looks like we got his trust. He has sleep. We cut his apron bows away miles into wilderness. There are no eggs answering. So who hears our faith to return? Stays this silent pace? When he knows, when bawling will we come back. His rags are whole-bound again. He won't talk much with a mouthful. Believe his getting-on sense should we strike water so that he may gentler us. Can't charm forever by smile, for wanting certainty.

THE KITSCH GIRAFFE

NOBODY LISTENED to me. Nobody wanted to go home. All we had—all we had ever had, according to them—was the giraffe. They loved it more than the sturdy home I made for them. For several days, reduced to camping out in our station wagon, relying on the convenience store for meals and washing up, my wife and children hovered near its hooves, stood underneath its pre-molded torso of fiberglass, and pondered the mysteries of its empty head as I watched. Telling them this vessel was false bordered on pure folly. A trucker from Texas tried his luck, first with amazement, then with f-bombs, but he could do nothing to prevent this spectacle. It had seized them with merely a sunbeam glinting off its yellow neck. Did they want me, the father, to stay in the picture, or had I lost my place to the giraffe? They considered this carefully. My feelings were at stake: I did, after all, drive them to the giraffe. I deserved some adulation. They insisted on waiting for instruction, however. An animal filled with that much kitsch must have a message. My wife flagged down drivers to have them lay Spanish candles before it. My children began constructing messianic chants out of doggerel from comic books they bought in the store. We would wait, they proclaimed. When the police arrived, they set up a cordon to safely demarcate our area, later arresting me as I tried to ram our station wagon into one of the giraffe's leg. Let me save my family, I begged the officers, can't you see, can't you. Sure, we see, buddy—you've got yourself a beautiful giraffe here, you oughta be proud of yourself.

DREGS

A FEW DAYS before he died, he said to me, "I'm never cleaning this cup out." He took it off the table and placed it in the cupboard with all the clean dishware, and there it would sit forever in filthy repose, if I believed him. Since I didn't have the opportunity to find out if he kept his word, I nearly asked his family at the funeral if they had come across any unwashed coffee cups when tending to his personal effects. Nothing good would've come from that, I figured. His sister seemed overwhelmed by the number of inquiries made about him, his failing health, what manuscript he had been working on, why his wife had taken the kids and was nowhere to be found, why he ended it all. These, I thought, were good questions. Over the next few days, I felt incredibly foolish for my boiling down in memory all the pleasant moments spent with him into an unclean coffee cup. That cup had meant so much to him dirty, and I was there. Did this also mean something about me made the cup so important, then? Sometimes, however, I think that had been the day he decided to give up. It wasn't worth the hassle anymore. He was letting it all go, and it wasn't important. Apparently, neither was I. It will be an adjustment, but I'm willing to have other people understand less about me if they stop asking his sister so many questions. She's not skilled at creating necessary distractions for herself, as much as I'd like to tell her this.

LITTLE MEAT

RAYBURN TOSSES me the claws because there's never enough meat in them. He's sad and lonely in southern Louisiana, having been promised by his cousin crawfish big as Maine lobsters, though now he grumbles over and over. In the park, the weather is mighty fine; in the calcified coffee pot filled with briny water, a lone survivor from the cauldron keeps its claws up. Rayburn looks into both and keeps saying, "I shouldn't've came here," loud enough for the Thibodeaux clan to perk their ears at him and share a laugh over another transportable cauldron they're shoving away in their flatbed truck. I want to show him. I have the idea to rip a claw open and show how a little meat can work, approaching some sweetness if he'd let it. The one in the coffee pot makes me feel guilty instead. I don't know what we'll do with that lucky mudbug, until Rayburn picks up the coffee pot, carries it over to a sewer grate, and dumps it in. Even the Thibodeauxs are long gone at this point. There are children on the swings with no one to push them, however, who Rayburn watches as he stands over the grate, while I walk over holding the smallest claw I can for him.

TEN TO ONE

ONE BY ONE they were all gone in an afternoon. They only packed two boxes, but not the withered houseplant. In less than three hours the house was dark again, unmade. For four weeks, no one heard anything else. Five movers visited but only stood outside, looking up at the red buds on the wild branches. Now, when six o'clock arrives, we are the last to stand inside. They reported afterwards that it must have been seven. Eight to a house, we knew otherwise, brimming with joy as they sung. And then nine months later. What they would think to see how we got our own home at under ten one day.

INSTRUMENT

THE TWO BROTHERS, somehow finding a buyer for their next-to-last piano before Berlin fell, also found a better peace in a nest of spiders playing inside what remained of their last one. This piano had never been used or even tuned: a showroom-only model the elder treated as he would a souvenir snow globe, growing fond of it over the years from its uselessness, while he regarded the younger inseparable from his massive ledger, despite there being nothing left to write in it anymore. He had meant to ask him about that. For as long as they could remember, the elder lived in the nice room upstairs while the younger kept the subdued basement; and, with both brothers closely equidistant to it, the piano held them in a fixed orbit to each other while the building crumbled within the city, the younger withholding the obvious question, *When do we sell?* It was not to be asked aloud by either of them. The piano was the first and last thing they saw each remaining day, the only piano left they could find a buyer for, spiders or no, which made the brothers forget they were the last person they saw before retiring every night. In their respective darknesses, they tried to watch them, to imagine their graceful scurrying across the damp ceiling in silent multitudes. *They are good,* they both thought separately, *these spiders he cannot see.* While one brother slept, the other wondered whether some must fall upon the other from slender threads above, though each failed to sense a joy apart from their descent in his own room.

CHARLIE'S ONLY BODY

AT LONG LAST the guards find his body at morning call. Not that it would be difficult to find. None of the bodies he had left behind were, either. He gave plenty of interviews about them. Never showed any remorse. Then the tables turn. It is he who no longer walks or talks, he who sees nothing, he who is now nothing but his own body.

Implications of this momentous development in the cellblock take a few minutes to register.

Damn, motherfucker finally croaked, the Correctional reports to Superior.

Sun's out, boys, it's another day, says Superior, stick him in the cooler with his friends.

So his body becomes only a body in the backroom behind a cold metallic door. This they agree upon because he should've been a body sooner, if not for those judges screwing things up when he got here and letting him stick around.

Much much sooner, the Correctional corrects, hell that's Charlie for you—dragging his worthless ass with ours out the door.

———

Other side of the country, Charlie remains standing in his empty kitchen when he hears the news from a distant relative, also a Charlie himself who got the call from another Charlie. His family has always been a family of Charlies. They don't know why. Possibly because of a beloved horse with the same name that tilled the original homeground way back when. Or a patriarch's favorite bordello mistress. Speculation abounds. It is their only tradition. The mild, inexplicable stories.

Save the one true story everybody else knows.

He would like to admit someday to people he has the affiliation of the notorious Charlie name, and that's all. Until then he has bad coffee and worse dinners. He watches too many crime shows, praying for glimpses of the occasional unfamiliar but not expecting them, re-runs included. His bills tend to be manageable. Robocalls, less so.

What he doesn't have is a claim for his grandfather's body yet. He mulls the possibility over for hours with newfound purpose when the cable news networks jump in with their reporting. People in town have not been paying him much attention as of late. At least it would give him something to do.

The next day he admits to a lawyer (not yet retained) that he knows nothing of claiming a body. Why should he? In the ground they go, that's it. The error of his ways has been revealed unto him from television. He's here ready to learn the process. Almost. He shrugs and sighs when the lawyer brings up the likely absence of a notarized will. Brings up the concept of a protracted legal battle. Brings up potential unwanted attention for him at home. Maybe he ought to let it go.

But what if the attention is worth something? A body is worth something? Worth a lot? If this particular body was worth something to someone else? He could get a piece of that action, even if it isn't much. The only piece left which resembles him in the mirror, as he sees it with each passing newscast.

Charlie is not letting it go. This is family he's talking about.

———

Not reflected in a legal claim faxed by his then-retained lawyer noting his affiliation to the body: Charlie does figure he's inclined for sun sand water over there. Big palm trees. Authentic Mexican food. Sounds sweet. Yeah. It's settled. He buys an Econo-Class plane ticket. Books a bungalow hotel near the beach. Considers wearing a Speedo, with or without thongage. Starts looking forward.

A few interested parties commence being anxious as well.

Upon notice of a legal walking talking Charlie jumping in, they start up. I claim this body, a second person says (a wife, maybe, Charlie's lawyer tells him, albeit with a missing marriage license). No wait I claim too, I have letters from him, a third person says (The Official Charlie Fan Club president, West Coast Chapter). Also, an indeterminate fourth party waiting impatiently somewhere with little credible standing (vague threat by proxy, could be one of the victims' families or the IRS or a crank).

Affidavits are filed in a flurry. Multiple motions put into motion. This is how a body becomes his body again. Charlie's sticking around awhile longer. That much the Correctional corrects itself. Sure. They pretty much expected it.

By week's end a preliminary hearing scheduled for a half-dozen lawyers gazing out the window with their silent curses over getting stuck with this flea-ridden dog. Notes are swapped on the sly in restless anticipation of the body's release. What will these claimants do? Photograph it on ice like Jesse James. Prop it in the corner like the Elephant Man. Display it under glass like Lenin. A man of Charlie's infamy could be versatile for padding the income.

In caution of assuring all parties will have say without them saying anything yet, one motion in court prevails for his body staying in the cooler until they are deposed. I'm confident we'll sort this out, says the judge. All present lawyers remain good friends when they meet each other for drinks later. They don't mention the judge's ruling. They pretty much expected it.

———

Having to deal with Maybe-Wife, who swings into Los Angeles first on the red eye from Dubuque, proves tedious for the Correctional. Lack of skill with paperwork aside, she does not act like any sort of widow unaccustomed to death. She skips checking out the sun sand water and straightaway demands Charlie produced, to no avail. They oblige her in other ways for distraction. She remains standing in the cellblock with arms crossed. Correctional shows her: See, this is the exact place where we found him on that fateful day. They offer her a look. Everything removed from it, but there's the bunk. No sun, no sand. A trickle of green water running from the lip of a dusky, well-honed toilet. A pair of moldering sandals. They offer her those as keepsake. She does not take them. They offer her a tour of the backroom. As close as she will get to him for now. At the cooler she faces a metallic door with ID tag before changing her mind about turning away empty-handed. His name is spelled wrong despite its simplicity and what should be their familiarity. She almost blows up at them, yet she refrains in exasperation. The state has been in perpetual mourning, of course.

———

My my my. This is a new world. Charlie sees it all over the goddamn place the moment his taxi pulls from the airport curb. Then a bit later there. It. Is. Sun sand water. A full mile of so many living bodies sauntering along without a care. After checking in at the hotel he wastes no time. He has the sand and walks it with everyone, could it have him and, he thinks, his goofy pale skin. Seeing sand wills his body here a formerly unknown purpose in thinking it does walk well, though nearly falling as he approaches the ocean. The seaweed tangles him up easy.

While eating the first and best carnitas of his life at a restaurant nearby, he reconsiders his objectives in light of these minor revelations arriving in heat. He almost forgets about Charlie's body waiting to be claimed, the other claimants who don't deserve it. Somewhat startled when he gets the check for his meal, he almost forgets how Charlie left all those other bodies to their own coolers to be claimed by someone. Would it be reasonable if no one claimed him. More just.

Regardless, he decides, what's done is done. It wasn't his fault. Abandoning a body in a cooler makes no home of his better when he returns, too. Especially Charlie's body.

He doesn't leave a tip for the server. On the way back to the hotel, he buys a suitcase of inexpensive domestic beer. He has inclinations, but not much else. Plenty of sun left out on the balcony patio, which amazes him. He grabs a seat and pops one open. Full view of the beach. The same people he saw earlier on the sand remain a little farther away. No, he doesn't need to see their faces to enjoy himself.

———

Maybe-Wife digs in. She's a small, polished stone to Charlie watching her in the courtroom with her skillful lawyer, the kind that plopped out of an electric rock tumbler he had as a kid. Perhaps precious to start, could be worth something afterwards with a shiny veneer, but likely not.

On the other hand, Fan Club president backs out of the proceedings early, his lawyer disavowing the need for all these proceedings given his client's handwritten letters from the deceased. He seemed impatient, Charlie thinks, not much fight to him for a big fan of his grandfather. *A mystery for whom fortune does not favor*, his own lawyer scribbles on a notepad next to him.

At dinner Charlie wonders if his turn is next. He has carnitas again at the same restaurant as yesterday, and served by the same server, who stares at him this time both before and after his not leaving a tip. He wishes Maybe-Wife stared at him like that. She is younger than he had expected, about his age. Not the kind of woman to commit to a broke, elderly felon. This bothers him for some reason. Then he walks alongside the water, and as the view improves it takes his concern in another direction. By the pier, with its lights, games, sirens, he starts wishing for a woman's body to fall in with his own at his room, if only once before he goes back home. If he goes back—there, he thought it.

All this sun sand water. All these carnitas. All these claims. All these legal proceedings. Either the place wants him to stay forever or leave soon as possible.

If he was a body, would anyone bother doing the same for him?

He has a while longer to consider his options as the phantom fourth claimant fires their lawyer, then throws in the towel a couple days later. Maybe-Wife is not ready to concede. Charlie can hear her angry conversations in the hallway outside the courtroom. He starts taking copious notes about her on a legal pad with a fountain pen he finds on the table. Such a nice pen. Can I keep this, he asks his lawyer.

———

Maybe-Wife's lawyer argues in impressive fashion that the body, prior to becoming a body, did not have expectation of a posthumous legal claim for what would remain after himself, save for those who were affiliated with him at a considerable distance but seldom wanted to admit it. Not a single phone call. Numerous birthdays without a card sent. Maybe-Wife, on the other hand, has been devoted from afar. Attentive. Caring. Visited the Correctional often for the plexiglass chat. Did as many wifely things as she could under the circumstances of being married to a man like Charlie. Is stable enough financially to see to transporting the remains.

Hearing these details, the grandson may concede she appears to have been fond of him. To a degree. Otherwise, no sun sand water for him in those decades lost behind bars. Outside it was ever close to him. Close enough to make his susceptible mind suffer a fantasy? Make hers as a result?

He wouldn't argue the money part. His lawyer does not, either.

The judge grants a boon, thinking Charlie needs to see what he is getting himself into, logistically speaking. From the courthouse he is whisked away to the Correctional. He's nervous the entire time in the backroom. Banal small talk is made accordingly. At the metallic door, he tells them if he had this much sun sand water at home, he would die there a happy man. Honest.

Correctional grins at him: This is where grandpa chills.

The door swings open and the body rolls out with a thud. It looks cold indeed. His eyebrows are frosted. He's wearing cheap gardening gloves. The hands are going fast, the Correctional informs.

That night he has four quick beers on the balcony to help forget.

He watches the tide mark the shore break white. He starts shaking.

Retreating to his room he fuddles with these odd organ pipes of an antiquated heating unit in the wall. He sits down on the bed, not sure if it works. Yet a click whirrs, the flicker of a pilot light he had somehow started. A modest column of fire behind the pipes soon rises and warms him.

He briefly considers a foolish notion of finding something to throw in there until he passes out.

———

By the end of the third week, Charlie is learning that most bodies, as viewed by the legal system, are insistent impediments to speedy resolutions in general. He learns, too, they get more expensive as the proceedings roll on.

It is also not lost on him that Maybe-Wife is losing, and the losing is eating at her with visible annoyance.

He wishes she is more familiar to him outside this painful setting. A meeting would help confirm his sense that her claim is, in fact, stronger than his, with or without the marriage license. He even passed along his hotel contact to her through the lawyers, despite recommendations to the contrary. This can be smoother if everyone stopped being a total stranger enforcing their strangeness. Then he remembers from his crime shows this isn't usually the case. Friends and family do this same thing, stare down each other in court. Why don't more people give up before the gavel strikes, he wonders. When they do, why does this system keep refusing their complete and unconditional surrender?

The day she finally turns during session and they catch each other square in the eyes. It's not as dramatic as he had anticipated. She's tired of waiting, like himself. A pair of glassy looks in resignation is all the gallery crowd gets for a final showdown.

———

Judge enters courtroom.

Present audience comes to attention.

Charlie remains standing weary at request.

He is told he has legal possession of the body pursuant to a valid claim superseding all others as a direct descendent of the deceased, absent of Maybe-Wife's marriage license being produced for full authentication.

Does he still want the body?

Yes and no. He hates the yes and no but there it is Your Honor. He doesn't know whether he can properly tend to the body in its current state.

The judge asks if he is given the body now, what will be done with it.

Probably nothing too fancy Your Honor.

His lawyer interjects: Your Honor, the body could stay in its current location until sufficient funds are procured by my client.

Correctional disagrees: Coolers are busy expensive places, and we got traffic.

The judge does not argue. Too many bodies at the Correctional, not enough paying kin. No one stays in touch anymore, do they, Charlie? Wink.

No I guess not Your Honor.

And any body belonging to kin needs proper disposing of in a respectful manner, the judge follows up. That is you, Charlie, I'm certain of it.

Yeah sure that's me Your Honor.

Last-ditch emergency motion made by Maybe-Wife's lawyer to review the standing of Charlie's claim based on reports circulating recently in the national press questioning his parentage but denied. Parentage has indeed been established to the court's satisfaction. In accordance with state law, Charlie is next of kin, with the body to be released to him post-haste.

Maybe-Wife's claim is thereby dismissed. She cries while standing.

Court is adjourned.

Charlie has won his Charlie.

Both Charlies are not laughing.

———

Filled with morose triumph, Charlie walks back to the hotel with a tall can of beer in hand. A local youth crossing his path who is also thirsty himself attempts a claim on the way. Charlie says, No it's mine. Claimant responds by delayed affidavit that Charlie's a fucking cheap asshole.

He mostly is, he admits to Maybe-Wife waiting on the balcony for him.

She chain-smokes while hearing him out on the rest. He tells her this was all meant to be a learning experience and he has learned more than he bargained for. The body, he explains further, has proved expensive despite it being relatively cheap in other respects. Hoped for offers had failed to materialize once the cable news networks lost interest and moved on to the next big story. Not even an interview granted with the local weekly back home. Therefore, certain realities have been imposed on him. Certain long-standing customs. Charlie's body should get its due like anyone else's, he concludes.

She nods, and it appears she's not mentally correcting him. He's been corrected by other people in this irritating way before. He almost starts liking her.

Would Charlie be proud of his grandson for this act of generosity, he wonders aloud.

Well, she hesitates in answering, and never does.

He finishes his beer and starts a new one. Feels comfortable with business out of the way. You must've been close to the old man, he ventures with her.

Yes, my grandmother was one of the people killed, she says while stubbing a butt out on the railing.

Really. Why'd you marry him?

Smile that lit up the visitor's room.

———

This world of sun sand water has been so warm until dark, then that darkness will give way to blessed warmth again for yet another day. The organ pipes must stop their music. The last beer chugged. Wet towels remain uncollected. His dirty underwear is stuffed into the luggage. No tip left for housekeeping.

The body traveling below Charlie on the plane travels well, courtesy of Maybe-Wife. He's slightly more pleased about this arrangement now than after her offer and the concessions he made to secure it. In the cabin, he tries telling his rowmates about the whole episode of his claim prior to take-off, as if it is one of his crime shows. He throws in some embellishment: the brilliant, unconventional legal maneuvering he did against his lawyer's advice to secure the upset victory. For the first time, he is forthcoming about his affiliation with the notorious Charlie. But his rowmates resist taking the bait. The beverage cart coming down the aisle seals their ignoring him for the rest of the flight.

With no conversation happening, a private ceremony plays out in his imagination at cruising altitude involving Maybe-Wife's plans divulged to him. She will enter the mortuary dressed in black and wearing a mesh veil. Put an expensive English long coat that had belonged to her father over Charlie's orange Correctional jumpsuit. Add a little make-up she carries to liven up his cheeks. Slip on his feet a decent pair of shoes for strolling the next world. One last word to him before goodbye. None of these gestures changes or means anything when the body goes up in flames, he thinks, but maybe she will do them only because he wouldn't have considered doing them himself for the departed Charlie. Should he take this as a slight? He doesn't know. Why not let her, though. She's paying for it.

On final approach, he decides he will not so much as touch Charlie's coffin until she arrives in town.

———

He is rushing and unaccustomed to it, courtesy of Maybe-Wife's stipulations going wrong. The farewell scripture requires no small finesse under a printer's firm deadline. He thinks he has concocted a solemn passage he needs to satisfy her: *Forever the sun rises and sets by the body; will you as well not walk eternal with me?* Except it doesn't sound right to him. Not to mention it makes the departed Charlie out like Jesus, which had been the big problem to begin with. Fine, then. Hurrying he includes it in the program anyway, omitting both the quotation marks and the fabricated gospel indicator.

With ashes ready to be scattered by a non-denominational priest at a roadside creek that the departed Charlie had never visited and has no significance to the family, he is relieved at first none of the guests have asked him about the dubious passage. Not even Maybe-Wife. Instead, she offers a different blunt critique as the priest sends a strange, grey cloud of Charlie to dissipate across the blameless water and time immutable.

You don't resemble your grandfather much, she mutters standing next to him.

Charlie blinks.

A benediction finishes it up. Go in peace, concludes the priest.

She lingers around, however, and starts smoking under the shade of a lone tree. Waiting, it seems, to his surprise. Watching him closely.

He is unsure whether he should be worried or not. The guests are distracting him, too. These few relatives in attendance insist on shaking hands as they leave, yet they do not thank him for attempting a dignified funeral. He doesn't understand how they pretty much expected it.

ONLY IF WE HAD LIVED HERE

THAT TIME I'D caught Dad standing in the hearth so mad with an iron poker he'd be shrieking later in my sleep. It was a bird he couldn't scare free. Mom began groaning lamentations and he snapped at her, both already balding. Daylight fell down the chimney. Chirrups raining like curses. I remember this since it was the first body I knew was coming.

Dad made me watch while he struck fire. He stood the burn. The bird flew smacking its beak against his feet on the floor. For a couple hours, I called it Peepsy. It had a sty over its right eye—bright yellow, swollen, bloated flush-shut. Imagining.

With time still for atonement, Mom quoted scripture. She always found Leviticus for us all.

No one could say who started the makeshift graveyard. Swear it wasn't me. I'd see it through my bedroom window until I realized what it was. Then Dad put my dog and lizards in. Peepsy. No ferrets. A kid went there to bury his goldfish. He didn't come back for hours, and they found him in the reservoir, long abandoned, miring for endless escape.

In the evenings I'd want an ocean approaching, but it was six hours of manhole sludge after a downpour. Dirt got soft and loamy, fat with earthworms. I made a boy eat one. Told him to shut up because there wasn't any playground.

Street number 624. The last square. Dim cul-de-sac few
pretty cousins ever visited. Initials in cement—great for skinning
knees. One kidney bean-shaped pool drowning: Deveraux. Four
heart attacks and two-and-a-half strokes. Greer, Carson, Prentice,
Kurtzweiler, Henderson, and McMichael in this order. Beasley
survived his thing. The telephone wires were working that day.
Plus the in-ground sprinklers.

On weekends I avoided communion. Dad in his only Sunday suit
saw me come home and spat. He threw my baseball into the sewer.

The cold flutter stayed in my lungs, spread out.

I'd given a neighbor's kid a piece of my birthday cake. When he
took a bite, I told him he was going to die from poison. Yellow batter,
orange frosting. My favorite. Dad confiscated my videotape collection,
deluxe Swiss Army knife, and my hamster "Godzilla." Later a 1982
Topps Don Mattingly Rookie. Near-mint. I climbed up into my bunk
bed with a cold metal bauble in hand.

Brown August days were for watching Dad try working the Volvo
in our driveway. No amount of wrench fixed it. He came inside
to Mom and fastened the knob. But the damp drywall didn't stop
anything. Those, I thought, were their wet heads.

My best pencil drawing of me on top of a girl.

Dad coughed emphysema. Mom had to warn me about spreading
diseases.

No, not really. If she was there with me, she was malformed, a
phantom pre-teen. Some name carved into the boy's bathroom stall
marble at Catholic school. Tan in her underwear. A thousand thin
blonde fingers, now diving, now undersea, now sneaking up my back,
now with the waters. I swam to kiss her face. I forgot her.

Crawling into bed between Mom and Dad.

That was once how quieter evenings had started, but I wouldn't
be sure we were nowhere talking to each other in our sleep.

ALLUVIALS

PURE

HE BURIED HIS EAR against the closet door, on the inside, gleaning the sound of a flute—its humming bubbled in short breaths—that could scale low, low moans. This instrument played, after a blonde violinist, before a raven-haired chanteuse, as he refrained from coughing, preserving the disparate sounds fresh within.

The flutist did find him sick, sleeping like his father, though under a hanging of suits. She startled him searching for a sweater, the audition finished. His nose bled on a dinner jacket.

"What can only be the body if an emergency?" she asked, passing a handkerchief.

The boy dabbed. Not the stream he thought; and sometimes paltry specks would fall on his pillowcase when he awoke. Yet her cloth soaked the blood in a cloud.

She didn't belabor his ruining red. She winked. Whispered to him, "Keep it."

Windowless mornings lay obscure in drizzled rain. Pages of tablature turning yellow, faded, even while pining for sunlight.

In dreams he recalled a paleness which, as a child, had wrapped him in bedsheets so taut, no one heard his suffocating or saw an unstained mask of his face.

THE OTHER

"LET'S GIVE A taste. Give me in," he would say. There are some ways saying this, which he would not say, but it is too late. She tastes him. She gives him in. Instead of something she will not say in return, there is another taste letting her give her a him which he says in these other ways.

PAPER

I WROTE MANY, many letters to Mrs Sawana. They were all about the same in content and expression: *I belong to you*, or *It's something I said, isn't it?* In lieu of my signature at the bottom of the page was the orange dot made by the tip of my nose. My anonymity to all—besides Mrs Sawana—was assured. The stationery paper I used was common, untraceable, as was hers.

Write to me. Tell me who you are, she wrote in furtive strokes.

I had been following advice for men in a magazine I used to read. Thinking the gesture romantic (and, I vaguely hoped, erotic), I sprayed some of my favorite cologne at the end so she might recognize me later. When I was done smelling the page, I realized I had left a small impression of sweat where my signature would normally be. It dried into a dirty brown film. I took my business inkpad, pressed the tip of my nose into it, and covered the offending mark. The best work of all lovers is created through the concealment of accidents, I reflected.

Hana no in'kan: a nose intaglio. Orange ink, sebaceous. Elliptical circle. Tiny dots, the pores raised off the paper's surface. A signet? That was not my name being sent to her, nor even my pseudonym should her husband stumble upon her carelessness. That was the point where she started.

"My little orange dot," she whispered, directing her kiss to the edge of that piece of cartilage I took for granted. No feeling came from it. It could not blush on its own, so I did to compensate. I glowed, frightened and ticklish.

She had no such center of gravity. I almost didn't know what to do. Her body seemed uniform; each proceeding part responded the same to me as the previous one. Flush of movement followed the course of her blood and mine. She nearly flung herself out of my arms. Then she finally welcomed the rest of my body. The sun rose and set beneath her as she did so.

My little orange dot, she began, *we should have met sooner.*

I gave up wearing cologne once I learned what she adored. A childish joke we shared—yet painful in its simple truth—soon materialized: I brought a single flower to her each time, knowing it would have to be discarded that same day before she returned home.

Mrs Sawana, I wrote, *I hope to give you a flower that you will keep.*

A joke always becomes serious when repeated often. I considered whether to use better paper to write to her, with enmeshed flora. Etsuko offered to make a personal sheet for me. "What does she like?" she asked. Camelia, Azelia, Hydrangea. Blades of short grass under her feet, too, freshly cut. She had just the right mixture in mind, the appropriate texture for obedient fingers. "This sounds serious," she unfortunately added. Upon further consideration, I told her to wait.

The correspondence remained prolific and lively. My desk filled with letters, all of which were addressed to my favored olfactory peak. I remained confident that I was somewhere behind her words. When we met, I felt certain my identity was saved in her caresses.

The mark became the source of my pride. Every pressing carefully deliberated. After I sent the letters, I often forgot what I wrote.

She eventually did not respond to each letter.

My little orange dot, she replied, *is getting bigger. Are you pressing too hard?*

This letter concerned me.

I walked to and from the train station with my head down. I worried that the tip of my nose, perhaps becoming stained permanently from the ink, would give me away. I washed it with determination and looked at it closely in the mirror for diamonds buried underneath its surface. I buffed it with cheesecloth and cooled it with ice cubes. I took it for walks at night and let it lead me to her doorstep brazenly as she slept with her husband. I stuffed it with tiny balls of tissue so it could keep shape. I had the priest bless it at my local temple, who could not perform the service without a concerned smile. There are no sutras for the deliverance of inflamed nasal passages, he explained. We burned incense anyway.

Mrs Sawana, I wrote, *you are being served well, but not by me.*

I wasn't certain what I was waiting for, if not her.

I patted the space on the stone bench where she would have sat next to me.

The day grew late. She surprised me by kissing my lips first and only. Besides one more letter, nothing else followed.

It is over, my little orange dot, she wrote. *Take care of yourself, and that which I loved the most.*

I asked Etsuko to make the paper I had originally wanted, though she told me not to brood over the whole affair. I promised her I wouldn't. She took my hand for a moment. I said nothing. She left me feeling slightly guilty.

The paper arrived in the mail with prompt courtesy. About two dozen cut pages. It was bundled with a crepe sash that carried an invocation for the writer, which is the custom here among the papermakers: *Respect the pen, honor this paper, revere those addressed.*

Obeying the invocation, I waited for several evenings.

Mrs Sawana, I began, *will I have a name someday?*

EVERYTHING

AFTER MY PASSING ON an unexpected (and, I had thought, likely accidental) invitation to attend that same night a formerly renowned colleague's early retirement gathering thrown by his few remaining supporters in our department, I still receive a group email the following day from him saying farewell to us all, in which I am the first, the only one he thanks for everything.

THE MISTRESS

I RETURNED THE book two months overdue. I didn't know it was overdue and presumed implied innocence would work to my advantage if I had a sympathetic clerk, but, no, she turned out to be uncharitable. There had been an outstanding request: assisted autobiographies of politicians' mistresses were in vogue, so I owed nearly twenty-five dollars. "I could buy the book at that price," I complained. She agreed with me. "Why don't you pay the full replacement fee," she said, "and you can walk out of here with it." Twenty-five dollars was too much for overwrought passages about secret rendezvous at Martha's Vineyard and some vague philosophizing about infidelity, especially after learning I could enjoy myself in other ways. I can be frugal to no end—except only for me. I think the clerk resented that. Tapping the desk with her manicured fingernails, she snapped my wish fulfillment in two. She was going to get my money one way or the other.

PASTE

PASTIEST OF SEVERAL unrehearsed faces used for bowling the reunited men in her life over (and almost flattening them floor-smooth in the bouncy transfer), this rarified expression she now hoards for distinctive, inelegant squabbles when theatrically nonplussed, or put out of her sallow skin, while counting to herself spoken conjugations of *horrify* as relating to many ill-conceived gesture apparatuses—specifically misguided, the confetti surprise he attempts upon her return home after tasting the wrong hors d'oeuvre, an asphyxiating ladyfinger mass-produced in a dubious Chicagoland facility processing tree nuts rife with her least favorite histamines, which had triggered premature Blueface, then resulting in Redface of striking emotive vigor following the failed ingestion which was, by and large, coincidental with an esophageal fiendishness his Turtle had come to agitate and expel all over the impenetrable Feng Shui she had self-energized—however appetizing she may appear to him while he stirs in sweeteners with wide, thorough circling.

MIDDLING

OFTEN, YOU'RE DRIVING me where I know you don't know where you're going. Unless we're in a tunnel. "Let it ride," you say, "we can't get lost—either way, out the other side we go." "Or we stop in the middle," I add without thinking first. You can't fathom why: no one stops in a tunnel, of course. You can't remember the last time you saw a car break down in a tunnel lane as well, forcing its occupants to walk the remainder. I also imagine tunnels, like this one, have perfect operating records in getting people to the other side, no matter what. Even if they walk it. Only problem is everyone else zooming by. Because they know where they're going. They don't—and can't—stop until the other end; do the walkers wish, however, they had turned around while they keep walking ahead? Don't wish for anything in the middle if you can help it, I'm about to say before I recognize which direction you think you're taking me.

PLURALITY

THAT SHADE OF HER, coming to a clear and only again. That setting down, sitting down, all around of her. The good sport. She would set the table and I would make the meal. Long before that, I made the table from beams of wood and she set the meal elsewhere away, somewhere off to the immediate side of her side. If we ate that meal, it was while I worked and she ate with someone else inside her inside—hence the third person indeterminate. One uses the fork, one uses the knife, and one uses the reflection of utensils against each other, caught in time sparingly for the evening light.

THREE HUNDRED MILE HOUSE

SHE CALLED HIM inside. Sometimes she'd call him in again. Had
he seldom been welcomed by anyone, he would've left her younger
when done. But not now from many looks of him on site. Limp, angry,
worn—he had them parceled up there in a lockbox without lock.
Some screw bits. Wire cutters. Little gadgets for occasions not worth
the advertising. This sure was the place. He wondered was she used
to making mistakes just standing around on the threshold with those
almost-sunburned toes. Poking out for this guest shoddy he couldn't
bear asking anything of her—except one name, naturally. All about her
that leaned against him said Who was waiting for Who Else. That's who.

———

Deal. By noon. He held up the screen door: a contractual obligation
they didn't dare breathe to speak. It had already been spoken. She
christened the lightbulb on the porch his *in-vocation*—which he
considered his job fixing. He also thought she make-believed her word.
Didn't let him bother. What was he waiting on then. Had *out-vocation*
before her days upon moving here with promises. Could've been much
longer. Still her wages of a maybe warm spell, staid comfortable, a
few meals. Any other sort. Take or leave. He knew the decision of
a man's ruin either way. A week ago finding motel stationery paper
he'd written back to town about how he couldn't help himself but

helping others, the Golden Rule, yes, sure sure, there'd be another, there's always another, he was getting along. Or getting along was what counted better.

———

That was her tour: a kitchen he guessed. The rest later. "Later," he assured. Winking she seated at the dry sink with the brush of her hair. There hung piercing slips of a finger in his belt loop on his jeans when her tiredness started or startled him by crow stumbling outside on a branched bit, tethering its meal to single beak, and kept alone. Otherwise, nothing afforded a view. The floorboards chirped. When she stood up the hallway akimbo, he could see her easier squinting. Then she could see he didn't believe her about being much. Was terrifying brought in with little short of a warning against and be beat to it. He didn't even know if she knew a father. Likely sent himself away long time after these rains kicked up and out though he had gotten burned on likely before. Just him looking for the switch again. Good property to settle away from the open. Sometimes they told him so in town following August.

———

These things to him took time because she liked them a tad ornery and anxious before coming. Kept strained peace but for the back of a hand once. The dresses always proved it, not a single rip needing a stitch. Certainly no buttonholes with a nosegay for her lone exception. There were few alterations with little extras inseam when weight slid off with his creativity, him thinking of bells, tiny melodic ones, that'd rush her from dining room crate and outside sucking in earliest air. For a while it was the bed helping. He fidgeted with a handsome spring. Seemed on the other hand he didn't really hitch all the way from town to whip up breaky-fast. Had been a short order cook for a few months because the lie about Eggs Benedict. Watching her change he said, "Cook you eggs ev'ry day but no sauces." It was fine. She ate them plain as could be. "You sure how pretty I look," she asked around his shoulder, her freckles turning out too proud. He grumbled, "We're eating here," fork in hand. Sunny-side ups from saddest coop he could expect. He reached for an empty pepper shaker if to shush her only. Breeze other way through windowpane like the big goner. A home's had enough, he thought less than careful.

————

Even at appreciable distance, empty tractor stood out waiting to stare at her holding his hand sweetly awkward. He wasn't surprised. He saw *No Trespass* had posted signs at its inconvenience. Gates still on arrival. Tilting signs she wanted to know was the warning really him. He shied away and set looking over. He'd realized a new community never too far, already entryway walls put up and out by the long road to town where he had walked in. He evaluated foundations laid, skeletons making shape, one story, two stories. There went the concrete of the future. Bobby Jo and Sara Jane would sure get their grassy set all right. She finally told him, "Don't bother." She'd been around before and found their tools lying. Picked one up at a time and dropped each to see how far noise traveled from her in a house without walls. Soon a collection of hammers and nearly a thousand nails as near as he could count lined on her fireplace mantle, all the pointed ends pointing towards him. "Welcome back," she explained happily for a change.

————

The wonder of trees had them hidden well-off and she slipped her hand below his waist holding it at the soft flush when she started hearing water instead. He grew impatient. Said her blessed be damned. But this terrible stream wouldn't let her go, not quite yet with drowsy sun on the line. She, in some circumlocution of her telling herself as if, remembered nearly drowning in it because as a child she thought it still enough to ankle through, her failing to see shadows in the rocks hide deeper spots. He was playing her to show it all—if she really knew it so painful. She was asking for trouble. He'd been around horses before. In such a tussle there'd be one bruising foreshadowing others, but he could've asked

her not to take it to heart and that he couldn't go back until they had
his bed made up. Privileges lurking about this world if he'd let them
happen. She'd get them sooner with him in the mood for smarter.

———

Already getting flat with pent-up energy, he fooled her thinking
magnetic waves made this planet—any planet—spin fast, pencil
drawing a linewise course on the tabletop through a near-perfect circle
and making dotted dashes in bending vectors like the circulation of
strange woeful powers that no one, especially him, could explain so
perfectly without the hesitation of many years' experience. When he
was done it had its sense. Somewhere out a ways, he pointed blithely
into relative space but starting to plot out stars, was the grandest stake
pushing us—who knew where we would go following it. And she
moved to the very edge of the table.

———

After her her her it occurred to him she hadn't let him watch dawn creep
up the length of how many miles it stayed away. A window faced in this
direction and, in his head alone covered by bedsheets, a slightening fear
of two other white houses that split the construction site horizon. Only
because were there neighbors who watched them while together—though
he'd spied no one. She left the window open in full view of another
window not far away with lace curtain across their movements buckling
throwing each and other, the pane propped open with a cleaned tree
branch, initials whittled into it. He'd studied the letters. He didn't ask
about those. "Too hot closing it," she whined, coercing agreement. No
matter the distance this sun hadn't stayed far away enough for his liking
her. He jammed the branch back into the pane, his thumb crossing a
series of carved J's and M's. Not since arriving here did something fly in
but wasn't as if he didn't watch for it day or night. In between she slept
quiet enough. He crawled back. He didn't close his eyes for amusing her.

———

Old well was safe racket she had going nowhere. Taps in the sink dried up—he knew water rerouted for the new houses but humiliated for her he wouldn't say priority. He watched her carry that wooden pail with both hands by iron handle at her chest as though this would get special. Second childhood. She ran out to the field while she could. A group of stones covered by wooden planks nailed together. He scratched his head. Anything could fall through. If something did she didn't care, it was for imaginary flowers anyway. He thought he ought to help haul but decided not. He wanted more for her because this might save him explanation. Watched her lower the pail down by rope. It went real smooth. She called out to the water like a scared kitten under her sofa. Sadly taken by two prayerless hands.

———

The room in thirds had no door. She said to enter he needed to make one. He thought out outlay and design and loadbearing all the rest but couldn't come to any conclusion. Hadn't the saw either—town hardware wouldn't let him buy. Windows pardoned next and not spoken of without her asking "So good morning?" this time. Lots of plans. She wanted a library of splinters.

———

She lit a candle, then the newer bedroom. Ran match to her fingertips. From it shadowlight reflected in boudoir mirror she stood in front if while he undressed self-consciously this time since she didn't watch him do so. He hung his jeans on the tip of a bedpost which he usually did whenever a bedpost loomed there prone to the moment.

———

She didn't begin at a gesture. Followed slow-toting beetle on lace curtain with a glass eye in her right hand. He wanted to her to kill it and get started. "Make you regret," she glanced at him, "you'll never sleep sound again with anyone 'cept yourself." Turning back she squashed the beetle with her other hand streaking the curtain. He had to laugh. "You've conjured me away now," he imagined himself crying sincere.

———

That faded crimson a body can leave in so many places and why not, why fucking not. Before her returning him a lain motley of scars didn't lessen what was building out there to spite her. Just dirty under her fingernails. Broken flower stems she wanted to pick green but nothing asked a touch. Then another sun rose. He felt one of his letters unsent grazing his forehead. Threat to some. Foreclosure to others. Wouldn't send post-haste and get involved. She'd find a place if not here. Probably came down between her and her hallway as it did sly. He craved recalling that how look.

———

Some stretch up the long road drew a softy. Always wore designer sunglasses, he'd noticed, and throwing his duffel in backseat told driver where he'd like to go but also willing if it wasn't the rightest destination. Driver responded in kind it wasn't the rightest destination, so he had to listen to this guy on and off. There carried surly grandkids and inclement weather patterns and politicians and politicians who needed tending to before three hundred miles about dried up into a obligatory thank-you smile in the last few meters pulling in for gas. He gave the driver his remaining dollars. Yeah that's hello been said in these parts.

———

Siren down his street woke him too early before a shift, something resembling what he'd heard before elsewhere. Surprised him same sirens on the outside meant different things, tornadoes, fires, even the occasional air raid. He chuckled. That'd really straighten this town out. He got thirsty but decided staying that way meant not wanting to stumble in darkness to the sink for a glass. Meant staying. Easy hours pondering how rainfall in his room would turn him over instead. The sweetened relief and its approach more so. He kept never having to get up yet.

ROOMIERS

SOMETIMES—NO, I can't bring sometimes here. Let us say tenant history stays where we put it personally. It's too personal. It might also be coincidence, but I'm not one to believe coincidence, so I am the only one.

Naturally, this is how our fin de siècle adores its own appeal. It's the best perfect age emptied right.

Or does my brownstone make me worrisome?

Worried people, like me together with him, could be further pedantic. This happens by compliments from him handing over fountain pens (I was doing so well!). Consider if I faint with his clipboard: "Oh," he will hem, "call my office again tomorrow morning." I think he hems wonderfully, and sputters, too. He makes a cozy parlor while I tug at his better leg. He doesn't mind his tie plastered with restoration particles, either.

I can tell you they ask me not to brush them off. I need more familiarity with parlor etiquette. I do converse about pristine ambience, and it won't appear unbecoming for a while.

This space is about a Victorian ceiling fan, I try his seedy patience. Backdrops where neighbors suit themselves are featured. Freshly lacquered wooden floors. Impressionable appraisals. This candor.

Initial disclosure: the opposite end of that hallway is where I may grow a bit roomier at him.

THE OBLIQUE ROMANTIC

THE VARIETY OF passers-by all hot and sexy for being nameless is not rich, though here in West Virginia alone I purport seventeen documented types, including what I call *Lappers*. No state agency can correctly identify the first and last ones, however. Those are left to my own devices. They took days to help. Which is why I enjoy being haughty and overrated and ruined asphalt patches over cobblestones simultaneously. Please save me saving them all. In the official version of events, shame led me astray from true love. Candles also have a confused end never burned regardless of the impersonal threat of idiosyncratic winter. Knowing that: do I tell people how cold it must be outside before someone considers dying of exposure? When you have me arrested later, you'll know it wasn't worth the proposition vote you stayed at home for. Hey. I mean you shouldn't be paying attention right now.

———

Endlessly I get myself best, I tell an unrated extended version of her (I suppose), wanting to thank everyone who helped though with a few choice names left off because, she notes with coy precision, I'm a big goddamn asshole who makes her fucking cry so fuck you okay. I had written in an overmarked college textbook, *Our concerns must be larger than ourselves.* Theory: I think I pulled a simple grudge with this noise well behind me. My unintended victims can be identified at the grisly

forensic scene from idiomatic degree of limp smiles. To scale back local
murder rates, more therapy sessions should be held in basements; that
way, there would be humorous consequences to acting stand-offish.
Theory: the rules of engagement, as they must apply to all perceptions
that are inherently false at the start, lead to no real engagements. If
this follows, I will have no recourse from studying her anti-domestic
dialectic on a weather-beaten porch swing. She's in a league above or
below me. Don't matter which, y'all.

———

Listening to her describe description makes me a greedy patient of
my own disreputable philosophies. As the ornate nature of detail itself
renders nothing at all, I will at least have semblance behind her—a
sunset, for instance. The random angry populist mob descending from
the alley takes me calm, then. What I promise to them upon my safe
return give its first mediocre symphony in the shuttered downtown
amphitheater: just another failed teenage prodigy. I scoop her up
with hands while I can. They are a challenge to find. Someone asks
for a moment of your time, and you'll always know them by sight
afterwards. Trains keep derailing with an impassive shrug. Photos of
each crash scene demand carrying my pace along a current that the
Ohio discarded out of boredom. I know I shouldn't live this small
among the flames. How fucking lovely, she says.

———

That little works as it should anymore has the fearsome nostalgia of a
fictional war-cry. House numbers are lost in the unsafe dark. Prodigal
sons buried without jokes attached to the ironic eulogy. A new park
opens next to another park; no one gets to decide which is better.
Rambling replaces the essential discourse of speculating. Let me have
an idea: to speak henceforth to her is to pretend. Cleaning up from the
flood that devastated this town in the 1930's will take some time but
this is our home and nothing can make us leave it. Approving wink
from an airplane passenger far above in business class is also a regional

commodity built on mutual trust, entrepreneurial initiative, and cooperation with goodwill charities. Tell me you can't see it. Go ahead.

―――

Babies abandoned outside, swallowed whole by rabid ferals. Neither traveling very fast saves the governor much embarrassment in the run-off. How epidemics work: An intersection of casual negligences and oh look how cute is this. At present I prefer keeping her safe from them because it sounds about right. This wasn't my backyard when it could've been my backyard. Hear one door, try the next. Sameness becomes pedantry avoiding similarity. No one is going home with a brave handjob tonight. Around every corner is another every corner so get a clue already, shitheel. Why ruin perfectly good explanations for lost privilege. Save those to defend your famous self. Even I can fabricate the words from a letter I wrote, down to the day I failed to send it.

―――

After safe dark, with her sleeping the pretend sleep, that long long walk in one of the parks can fetishize me for the strain of my imaginary greatness not performing. Often I expect to find blithe, fooling couples emulating Emily Dickinson, others exulting the vital warmth of friendly poultry, a cheap suicide hanging from the footbridge with an unused condom in his back pocket. But I don't enjoy it. Any of it. Jesus, they're all just like me occasionally. Mark well where inappropriate laughter keeps at bay for the presumed break-up. I, too, am forever turning imminent, but good luck being scattered over the place when too sober and not as alone as I require. It still surprises me that my grave could be so shallow, Em. The animus of a certain path may prop up my resolve, though will it put me where I should be with you. Such as under a cornice. Right. I remember, as a child does, how only obscenity accomplishes itself the easiest.

NATURE

SHE ARRIVED UNSURE about being here. I put her at her ease during dinner. The candles, she said. It was the only difference she needed, but I wanted her to see more.

I took her out back to view the statue up close. She didn't seem impressed. We walked down to the dock. She was bored completely. I showed her the old stone well not far away. She wanted to die.

Throw yourself in, I told her.

———

He felt the disappointing pause.

"So that's all that happened to her?"

AUTUMNALS

A VENEER IDYLL

on parch of laketide
a cupola shares— wherefore
has it been sent
                where,
                        he asks
or else savor concealment
upon his concluding part:
do believe otherwise

middle lament
the quails sing
petrified in must be twilit,
a tale taking one
readies her bearing

Amongst lowgrounds arrival taps shoulder. A perpetual bed yet his.
Will see he is. And be known then. Seedgrains before had read script
from saving hands' breath together upon veins grazing. Wind grows
earthen chaff awake. Its many causes store bindings done in grounded
stitch. The call when pages recite what may split abundance into tune.
Rough-hewn melodies heard pasturing out the lengths. Into former
lore should he distance over speech mislaid, tidal and come far enough
rising twice unnamed. Verse origin this sudden can attest to. Aboutface
tosses offers of supposal lands only. Creation around nonetheless so
rewards fate encumbered at neglect for sending praise that this world
must build life without.

Give in the lane buckles under newer oxen. Ditch tosses possibilities over fringe. Into circumspect dressings lace themselves with remainder lined. Over and through fatty webbing scrapula brainpan eyeleak and liptail—hastened coverings, the design of another sentience to be encountered. Those roads had held onto him. They would press together clay and rough dirt, saving vector in thereby. Not yet a hallway guiding the traveller home he had resisted seeing. A toward for culling whey. Chaff in secret which stores autumnal torments.

Spinning elliptical does jasmine mingle him throughout with deadest breeze touching. Little else holds in metered space, a keepsake succinct he fashions himself out of shores battered, but insects hovering close to attempt the impending warmth of same. Should he find no discomfort, they lay their eggs into him. Germination arranges pouring away its source as apocrypha will not prevent a feast upon blood: these shimmering inequities. Past coolings surface from benefactor's tumult and pain, free to wrench away drought in a hailed cradle stream. Then into divide carves his canyon. All else is imminence unseen. What flows to the dirt, so he has read, wheedles broken grasses beside the young river's firmament. In too many granted years a golden apple signals blessing prolonged. Growth by these foundling grounds soon concludes this lore among others of the inchworm's soft tooth he will someday forget.

Nest of specklings across does powder blue dilute. Spotting enrages his walk alongside. Shore illumed thereabouts skim. As well a stir often unusual. When brought, few entities touch these bywaters, save winged insects spared reflection. A sunbeamed limb angling trees from their succumb over moment's inglorious. This redress will hazard. Sleeplessly presuming that always is everywhere. Teemed lilypads stay consulting their shelter, the lapped tenants underside. Each terrace intertwines slow breath scuttling past. Same basin for one another. With darkened maw of hearts gesturing, a yawning subaqueous anew. Shuffling forth the skins through filmy reaches never coveted. They do not stand opposite themselves stretching: all had seen this same expanse once harbored prior the Great Eyelid blinking approval. They persist sending corpses.

Cut along a lamb masters the knife, the single quail he keeps alive.
Making skein and meat bespeaks a failed attempt of them together:
one watching, the other delivered. Into as up toward his hilt may come
across its own steering, heretofore breastbone and riblets in the heat.
It cries unsightly before farther, moans for dear settling in the soft of
another's hand cusping its seal until time is drawn.

Verily,

he says first,

then falls what decides for him instead. Nevertheless lessens the knell
of deign-work, yet it does not twist his blade's victim towards crate
collapsed over straw. He should know himself gentler than this bleating
expiation, perhaps ever more so. The slough of its refrained feel blessing
him as he struggles. Its warmth in volatility speaking in avian for the
caged friend. The beam nailed into place hanging the stripped away
entails him apart except. He gives his quail unnatural sleep by cover.
Rust spends its ancient hue underneath much more than lamp-oil to
the dying restless, little less than a reliquary of the corrupt strand he
slices away from himself.

Brief nostalgia carves on turn of skilled wrist. Debased, the open cavity
hangs on his three-arm length of rope. Slung the knife's shackle, it
foretells. Fresh ribcage bides his design to become a canticled doorway.
It pines and melts into his abdomen for safe keeping; and in abdomen
does dance swallow all prayer, falling for worms to pluck up. Recitation
would have the plain rend itself, save the insects' thirst mustering their
speechless suffer. Perhaps he wishes to plant there, for them. Birds also
have their escape as singing assemblies must succumb to. As does his.
Lining his interior, a paleness in suffocate planes these manners across
his marble slab. Here or held on even waist recalls the First Felling
by man. The resulting distillation owns his heaven's affront. He asks
serving no more despite these beasts that rest within trudging reach of
his home. Yet he must provide them an outside. They pace there into
beatings under the body's folds, an entire year spilled from unseemly
gullets that crawl the ground, and open their throats blanched by dust
they beckon innate.

Havings have him bear heaved odors done. Save or caprice writhing of inside those. A wetland enfold trusts him. Fowl milling about diminutive tastes, already interminable owning. The feathers pluck relent. He will remove shortest yet wills unworthy. Over ember-glow mocks their steaming aside: another has performed here. Better than his ever. Kindling it searches namelessly, mottled indulgence blends maggots this palest flesh. Then humility blunts obliging coarse. Only so able. More removes easy deceit. Finger lay thrust into cleft-groan otherwise it does not abscond. His trace majestic with carnality asking. Should care hold his game to mudwater scent and flame underneath answer by prompt grasses eating, there must be accounting what tongues may make pleasure—if single word escapes intact. Since resemblances seize lungs to a pierce resounding away partaken where.

Cautery shines without sail. What it keeps, in portion. Lineage places
the same to a fine askance stabled. Sharp muzzles. Teething groans of
past shadows slivered in stain-beat. There, too, are the slippery cords
studied often. Massed under black for chaff separated in advance.
A slide done, this one, her. Hindquarters etiolate their bellwether
selves. The more smells are steeped, a ditch will be lined with its pile.
Shame awaits. Some thirty ripples of sidereal he follows ask otherwise.
Maybe set aside the lives of ten-fold foals so they grow on thistles and
milkweed. Giving this a plained say for no one, save him, he rends
vapors made equine upon return. Their soft to the toothed comb
lasting. He observes them still at a hand's pace.

Apology smears clandestine blood to enjoyment. Provenance without as
a canopy. An offering up open to his kill. Any mercy allows quails some
suffering before expense. Left caught in the month younger as ancestors
had way by mistake. Including the frail thereby should their day spare.
Would meager wishes be satisfied under his cover but determined. This
hunted crave. Heaps of cunning pile by doorstep. The feeding upon
for swell until pillars buckle. How he gives them study. There is airy
weight in sensing hastened breath must lead shallow, the ample ruses
the flighted ply unforgiven.

Ossuaries, of immediate resolve for reining in antique landscape; of circumventing previous airspace demarcating property against goose carcasses, which prevent smelling when approached quietly. Unless the offense of arbitrary demise. He kneels. At eastern cry he already stealths them, having failed to assuage his home. Applause meets sky. Bending he shakes away their parchment and hoards. Hides scraps underrock. Circular reaches that had fanned beneath them now dissolve litanies. As though they had known,

There do I stay.

He retrains to uphold. Skins trimmed bleached stretched forget their place. Ashen heather guesses them as shape: fashions of quill and ink. Pin-prickliness their strata. A treatise that vellum overcomes upon force, and chances a damp hole some ignore in the morning. Him especially. To his smothering mind, ablution. A chant does not force skeletons away for reading later. Not while they are a degree colder from candlelight.

Greenery in the secret of their meetings, besting the foliage at
tunnelarches buffetting his poor garden. She is a sound companion
to his noons, bare and sparse to a single compliment of his only
leisure. Pictures being unwelcome diversions, his takers had been
taken in the night—by what he could not say. Although he, carrying
charcoal scraps in his pocket, sketches their life-portraits with seal of
beeswax, backgrounding a wisteria absent of its tendrils. His details
imbue instance. The smallest branch stripped by birds to leave quiet
grasp at the above air they control. Ashamed, she presses her toes into
reddened earth, watching her nails accumulate coppery grains. Will
her wondering always push like this. Her field sown upon another
field no more genteel. Nonetheless he instructs that the indelible land
will not suit itself, nor resist making memory at its own bidding.
Almond trees, for instance.

How human in their likeness,

he tries her

learning,

knowing the aromatic visages of the departed well.

In talon finery do ribbons come given a quaver from him, over upon
having her loosened in open, a spare cipher he pockets. Does lessen.
Deals with seedpod borne mid-air as blame. Forms sanguine and
twisting land toward for refusal. Suspension could attain from her
matriarch thought: possess blindness, reverse descent—albeit opposing
several delicious bounties. So it tries her, wets her arm unlike water,
seems pale for attempting to steal her indignity while he witnesses.
It keeps mingling. Wraps around her at the there she will encounter
later without his shears. Because, she reminds him, he landtrods and
still-births the same wrung startle he has tasted before. Another again
yearning solders him to backroom passage. Missing timber, it appears.
A healthy mire for a becoming color, one that pleases in the verdure of
every flutter spent. Hers. Which he has saved plenty. The fabric aggrieves
yet against. Lays inside. Her random scale, her perching gown. Intervals
of burlap mistake a devout wooden peg for any of his members.

Harm at its base lays warm to the sound of being said, heals soft
a threnody with alluvial expressing: hint. Only in copulation it
understates. What is reason to most. Either unto the his and the her
body, or deliverance expecting solidity relative to time remaining on
multiple hooves. So the their body not them. Harm's own relief—it
feels less personified than shameful here, in holding itself endwise over
their trim heads, since giving feeling carves godly out of them too
often. Yet all it asks for steals fluid into a mete and a dole and a parse,
which they could afford sunder for the very after courted in its wake.
Séanced as they speak,
                        Please,
                                half-dying removes pilled hearts from
burden of causing lockstep. Spread across entity or entirety such as.
Then harm deals these words underhand. It slips joyless into coupled
darkenings. By a thread they spin it continues to paint. Collapses
beside the tongue's root, this where bloodsteep grazes dreary any
bringing of silt they may have withstood.

The beast of a wing has but a feather to write with, this being
enough to share its telling. The how many hands she took, the know
of dying breezes. She has her hand. She has her hand on him, on
his chest, and his chest, and his. Laying there has her trading pieces
as moonlight cuts clear. The wellwater trembles. Sought mind spills
her meter—also what happened during her last. A posit slumbers
over prayer slighting into fold. The rasp of a pewter brush near
stones around her solders an entire tremolo to the ground. Sparing
a needle, at this point, favors curtains in imbalance. On her material,
raising supplants voice. In quaver do filaments spark over to crevices
she makes despite him. At peril: some darkness that slinks towards
them in echo. Their feet. Their feet shifting the ground dust these
floorboards. Each step creaks birdsong with intruder sign. As they
are careless being caught, they dare tendons flexing over their own
fibrous turn. She will be spent on the bale.

Released from bodice, day lifts herself. Brings bedsheets wound on arm into broken pages for an entire blinking, gone for sight and save. They keep dry under roofspan until a pitchered tray, worn with inlaid circling of watermark or melted vials, upturns the seal of fruits broken on her fingernail. He will settle for eggshells someday. Then, and not then unless. One hen has been parented from the coop, he discovers, and misses sunrise on its vantage. There is a salting left in the saucer placed by the door, another meal resorted to entirely over the insects' trill, their quivering life seeking. He licks the skin of his tip. The hall he finds has been dusted by night far inside.

Ornithology since veiled supreme retained her waking hours fascinated. A whir famished for joining at overhead flock: arrowtip pointed at equator moons, great blood sundry stored in wanderlust, taste of heat on tonguelash released. They had been lacking these epiphanies granted regardlessly in them. More an occasion of late summer months. So she followed. Something earned him at least. By her eye their migrations settled for entrenching warmer airflow beneath. And from the fill of every reason left them hemming cornices in celebration, wreathed banquet tables in steady wind. Awaiting daybreak. She will be much longer through. The middling lands yield many caretakers, perhaps a few sloped fields yet to be rescued. Those equanime children.

An unsettling sidelong vexed caring the lateness, having him delivered
upon vellum yet its dripping. Intent below signature. Save this being
a scenery, some speak. Tugged in the fisherman's boat, a knot of wood
out by a grave splendor. Fields crystalline at length. He bent toward
their muster visiting for propriety, sank lower on alluvial not entirely
concealed. And to gain, promises withheld. An honest man who is
loosened by the betrothed, patient bounds torn from wasted time
of searching little fingers, neglected had they gone. Those who stirred
fastidious in relief of other ancestors could only watch, not minding the
deeper plush of feathers garlanded row after row near their temples,
scratching. Had they paraded iron doors, enough false feet would
turn over clay vessels spent on center-tiles. Charred myrrh. Ambergris
premature after dusk. He was not spared simulacrum. Draping clothes in
scented hush, smoke warning of departure uncalled for.

Refuse open air,

they deigned,
lest finding ruined vanity.

Who among them listened once

claws of their smoldering pile tipped another hand. Reticent would she
come carrying her salvage across this trail. She grew in frame but a bit.
Expanse asked so furtively from her then on.

Hand-cloth'd her book stayed firm of vows previously as across him taking. Now without cloth—again. Brash enters the unspoken, elsewhere too late for her seasons. The coil either lengthwise within lower spine or opposite appeals he taught. This was a fancy splayed one slain out on flatrock, throat opened to notice his tuning. Soon giblets melodic. They bore sordid bleats in greased bowls she placed underneath, and the run-off collected. Offal struck her nose—sacred places keeping her child buried when he was not looking. In bin rolled eyes chalky white. The unappreciative. A gasp took shuttered side, stitching in her flanks. But his puncture delineated both. She heard him. What substance would she become in the blade, if left to it. What sluice her body flowed into before endeavors the left ventricle withstands. In private counsel her guiding tract. Growth, fruition, entirety. The host may better proceed to bathe along fresher loam. There it will bubble light moss. Expiation as pressed scents of tunneling flesh lost. With back turned she would collect these against his evidence forthcoming.

is not any page
that lips itself
a single band—
    sweet exfoliation
    vows solemn due
    had they sleepwalked
    been made, char and sting
    pending into mouth

Say a slip
and has she been
anything forward.
Nightbells
at three's wake thus.
Enticement rudders
palms underneath.
Slide past them
her surfacing.
Into empty assurances:
the lay of her price
shielded by him.
Yet does it save place,
dress her bassinet?
Following the very same,
in a lie sunk her clear
as a virgin circle.

An impersonal dress tries to make wife expecting. Fashioned for back clasp a scarlet jewel. Felt toward a soft in her spine of finger's well, what no naive bridegroom misses. Something holds taut, a string of no less enumeration than pearls those bedded wore dividing of shelled flesh their mingle. Only cause of sediment helps stir her. Does cotton hang soaked from her, a musking that staunches shoulder-wrap the clavicle weep. For her, then.

This hollow

responds kind shame,

he thinks. Sole bearer for a year leaves a stitch despising for him. As it was some daughter had cleared her womb out long before claim.

Malleable, these valences—orange peels asking what the next pare a thumb can muster. If not contrary, however, her veins splay themselves over spinning wheels, threadspools, or the crests of robins. Something she once understood left her numb to the fields, just patting on oxen horns. Perhaps the underneath is a crown on its way, its fancy white facing posterior. But presently as she is, silence demands open tendons for mares like harpsicords, peals of strings made on knitting eyelids, she speaks, pearls and knots and pearls. A test could boast better; and her fingers' reluctance portions out in savored jars, follows trails past the treeline where their hooks bend for lack of want. Pierced upon them, jousts for downpours too newborn, not sparing sundered gasps of cleaving beaks which keep their smolder. A slight burning makes them a home

or a burning slightness, as conscripts yield deaf aviaries. What
takes them on branches east of her face could not leverage.
Branching over gables, shared windows for their crib.

Some heavy

palette,
      he says, not entirely certain of colors, but thankful for night.
A child perhaps born in darkness: no great concern, though she argues.
Nest hung from ceiling beam. A redbird makes there, and, dispirited
upon its disappearance, flies headlong into windows days on end. He
notes its thrashing until its expiration on the overhang. He decides
against telling her. His nest-huntings often unproductive ventures
out past the lake into woods folding over each other, boughs of trees
linking with others, a blanket.

Scorched nestling half-alive landed on her shoulder, its sockets
drenched sable, rubies exposed inside of womb's shelf. Burial because
its mother's admiration. Every latitude and longitude spheres of air
concocted falling in afar hands. A cough lapsed from remaining den:
the betraying staircase. She scaled this sheltering province. Fatty
skeins lined the walls, peeling. Columned windpipes pierced by a
golden filigree (few candles raised stand against any heaviness), therein
breathing leaves anew she would have swum, drawing puffs of darted
breezes for eager stirrings. Did this voidance, fastened by copper
wire creased, need window. Not for wooden chair set out, padded
with stretched tanned leather. This resemblance comforted well-
groomed mares to seed, and suspicious she touched bolting trim that
prevented softer contents from spill. Then occupier provided rest which
extended arms unbending of leg's inclination. Where carriaged seating
commenced her in lake.

Staying lockstep in skeletal lights from afar allows the climbing of stairs where none have been built. Impassive lengths of safe infatuation seal them with nails. She counts squared heads dotting up, each crying copper for frailties that mar too many surfaces. Beginning with branches. What retains her station to highest steps not aforesaid. They are abandoned thick in the trained folds of her dress, leaning her over a reading pedestal.

She weaves sleepy holes into tapestry neglect. Silk for her threaded expanse purchased over unwelcome shoulder. Having at brushed daze: their guest by parade. Before them upon finding walls and the table-letting. To admire spaces for beauty. It is a bare creation thus. That fray draws beginning gazes as though hollow pearls thrust forward. There is also her question. Does crossing this room let the shadowdancer take thought. The benign ripple nervously attentive. Pinpoint light indents a harness slung about its edges.

Almost provoked by lambast heat, so goldleaf inside her shudders this din. Upon its curling scope kneels at balmy saltpeter. Base containment she hinges upon for furnace dwelling in neck, running fluid as falling from vertebrae. In secret cloak, a lamb underneath bleating her against. Pays snowveils over the heartslab it cannot reach for effort. Further consideration upon flays her lace. It bides guiled remorse. Whether fastened to crux or interred towards highest polarity could its face bite with smattering eyeteeth. A threading of letters seraphed dissolve into her yawn's handwriting. The scripting breadth declines contesting newborns ever their perpetual self.

Cauterized at will left no trace of flightpath or wingspan or eyegape or beakspread questioned expense of roots traveling underground while they sleep left pendants at their doorstep wept by design of acrimony lit corridors leading to trepidant dresser a surrender's pace from her ever opening it.

Insides of bird relegate secret well. A dianaphous of motley interments befallen itself, not likened to a mere cage but the pitch and strum of unaware melodies. Base forms to which numbers were inscribed: hen, cock, falcon, owl, seagull, crane. Dispatching these the hours—but how did such avuncular creatures fit into his house's scheme, its plumage already wracked with worms and other sucking mites, feathers split, broken, seemingly writhing in their flightless agonies begging some unknown power that be for release? His study continues. He gives up. Turns the bird loose outdoors—not to flight, of course, but to wind its way through country paths, away from its brethren, its wings glued to body in salubrious decay of their disuse until the whole of its body became slick, downed with sheen, the tail feathers long disposed since its direction was decided more by wringling of its belly and slope of its meager entrails. Lacquered fine by the sun in its boil, too many summers in their pass. It finally arrives at cool haven, its feet having fallen away and its leg bones worn to the very numb, so finding it easy to slide down into this expanse where the others have gathered.

Bypath as tribute pays sole visitation in an alembic. A perhaps festivus
resembles the yearling discerned, less favorable than soil gentling
past tree-lines. Had previous months not dulled implements of ruin.
On shoulder he carries these muddied inside. Treading cautious on
floorbeams unbalanced, he finds a newborn suckling. At her breast
tucks away surprise. Leaden hours had sullied the crying, she explains.
Yet tidings given—a son has crossed this threshold. The hope in turn
he would deal with other sons, know their minds and the stale orbit of
various concerns. As will vespers spring from impromptu altar, ceiling
dewdrops beam living its brunt. A carved chalice requires saving
this faulty rain. That night their child slept covered under glistening
meshes assembled.

Inclinations mindful fill groundhole once oiled straw is lit. Cold
knuckles crack, but his bleeding holds oblivious. Polishes as warmer
salve to supple pained sharpness—namely, roads that profess an overwhelm
of near-morning acolytes, load by load with sundries they carry. He weakens.
Puts himself toward them.

All in good manner of our material, ourselves

reduces

his obstruction's soft flap (if any benevolence be perceived). Not in least
steadiness he lets their knees have path-laying, drive posts into hard
clay. Their efforts yield a smoothed horse paying visit to innocuous tears,
and disassembling faith leans upon them unheeded. Then the spoiled
treacle of jawbone swells their din: they must vanish when fields return
in protest. Here preserved, he broods alone. Kindling muscle flayed.
Property forgotten in an elegant, imaginary knot. It now binds the
new devotee's affection fast. It heralds dismal kisses.

eyelidded heavy over
happen birds migrate
observe stringed progress
takes the stairs
fall silent inside
tomes sought circular
bookcase allowing
touch while sin

Tense of sullen pages turns
obscura collected
for his own eyes
(or his son's one day),
celestial substance
undertaken so needled
senses are flush. She paces
over many scripts—
until other shuffling
feet move her further
behind leafed curtains
he rounds this study with.
The décor suits
down to a thistle.
She has seen him
trim sheared roses
once handsome.

Roomless necromancy casts fey mantles filling incantation. Itself having eyes coveted. Hearth determines such by rendering volumes that close unread upon its builder: the ocean primeval usurped. Its prose however indefinite. He translates through limited syllabary, using an account of ordinary carp. A single utterance describes these carp, three syllables composed, similar to his speak. Used in other words. His sounds here and there prescribe an able story, one that authors disregarding further. Yet results delight him. He forgets returning to the preface which had resisted interpretation.

Why let hindsighted charms distract from profound depths,

he asks his zeal. Exquisite caresses ply this newfound fortune in guile. To blink ashamed is to not bear his own reward.

cauls roll together
on candletipped fingers
lower and poorer,
    let tarnished saucers
    carry tallow—
walls seep these
chance offerings

harvest
its channel
safe to place
dreading
for them at
a drift

Several thousand pages left, and nothing remains read anymore. Treating dictum blinds fleeting script while glimpsed underwater. Looping scripts of sand summoned from a belligerent childhood of wetnurses buried alive. Seraphs weeping from generous margin-glow. For him more captivating than statement proper. The light airiness gains another shortcoming. Skulled recesses of a narrator vanquish epic ballads of the inside-out chamber pot spilled. Should blame trample his effluence better, the rest curdles in larder with blackened spots to dig out. Overlooking them coughs away from her suspicions. Inclement noise profoundly suitable for his son's first tolerable words sprawling the floor. They are lain in tandem at the heel of his hammer. Entrapped so they would know no loneliness. Already visitors in hesitant single file.

Hoarfrost eats away remains at another despondence. Could his
fingers believe their slough: silvery-dappled pinfeathers backing down
in surfeit. Not enough fluid altitude. Drained pitch of peal from
telescoping winds. As he tries, he cannot read the dissolve below
tremblers of branches, these swirls about knockless, whooping whorls
colliding so enervated. But, shivering off slakes of watered skins,
must he forage to ever complete his till? Hardly does needing revival
ask. Sometimes a child's whistle will abound playful inside those
days remembering him dig. Load having his hands, awaiting hearth
underneath dangling spice-stalks when done. He stays in position.
He stays in this position. A trail moves up his buried interior. There
assume horizons, they who eye no wider than cobalt once woven into
the morn.

Spine seldom notices when grim toss serviced them. Affairs knuckles permeate less than complaints. Fourth column fifth column until endure this seated, her ears stopped with packing. Neither brusque nor plentiful. His willing bent broken on pasture hands. No different than with patience: the how many stumbling calves delivered however into dark cellar. Limbs moving themselves do please this whelp he escorts. Where seen to after by unbelief. And gathering the proper tenant is his vestibule indeed.

when great frost throes
take pane he defends no fire
expel breath form-melt-thicken
once at sacrifice moistured back so
secure by prowl alcove oppose
outside trees succumb an easily
wintered march opaque

she wakes him

> *it is pictures that have*
> *no such amusement,*
> *what sets ghastly limbs*
> *afloat in some penance*
> *I fear*

daubs her tears
similarly

> *I know a conch*
> *for colors cerulean,*
> *not infinite symmetry*
> *in a fountain*

icicle him for water his
cauldron into fall their
vanish geometer watch a
no more forthwith restive
as the perfect the

Alongside patience one spider-eye stays in a corner's warming greed,
coeval with its twilight hovers a tendril in mayhap inhabiting his
provided ice-pane. It holds tandems there, tunnels her even-keel.
Evaporates in watching above as airy hours. Close, the jostle prior what
studies its removal long. She does not bother as often as chases liken.
Trailing away silk screens, footsteps remain semblance. Hers behaved
if begged. The downy-fleshed pads a haul of obstinate. Just fraying
accord. Sear of untouched strings but for lent anticipation marks few,
is what bedchambers tell. Choice happenstance can seize, and will she
accept dearth as chests heave possession, several lifespans of a dress,
open shears' rusting for wedding hair. A vacant wardrobe sieves through
before then. Her lined tidyings shed meekly, a silvered glass until
pressing comfort:
>   *Many paths below many,*
>   little spinnerets
offer. How they do mind their sparse to taken women this well past
welcoming.

Glimpses train waiting at illusive enough they, each other.

Not any yet,

she disrobes. Because a layer should keep no carcasses, illumine on
her face absent lamps, commit a calm volition but to record them
these gestured pleasures. Hostile a delay will ask wintering glanceful,
Let stage her flesh,

and heavyhand with stasis their dim wonder, too
masked a feint. These spectators, in time, defame owning whitened
ground, her having newer partitions to settle soon—splendor blushing
past nuptial streams. Room day or night lengthened here about hung
limbs crowded, grasping. Some together men may negotiate false trees
for these stretches. As argued corpses they perhaps put out myriad
fires building her path. Behind them, walls serve spun drapery unseen.
Careless alter ages the so entombed. Then proscenium guilding takes
those servants away. Few ever give fleetingly under elusive attention,
she has inferred this bare.

Pithy is price given a landfill of spent husbandry from movement feast
seen. It overtakes her. They resemble onward like her the masking floor,
lithe pitches with golden swallows between feet's passage in urn. Her
slippers a question of cascades. Being pure tumult of. A neck surrender
which tears at shirts, their dismantled stitches piecemeal. She makes
her kind seemly, not a kept haunt to succumb least fell, but withal in
pausing. She whispers this world ripe forgiven. Roaming oversee and
be singled and she is. Bowing planks beneath her haven sample pale a
delight: honey due on drawn boughs. Or channeling amber, whereas
only seas could scry to redeem their own scintilla an eternity.

Elaborate snowfall there instructs uproot darkness earnest in promise, the always every abstract she laments. Wheeling cages mix her taking staged stream. Cured by drink, she stays inside. Their heads are next seething. Guess rears cumulative weight, duty more plentiful than pried. This inconsequence shut. Ground took them serious. Larder sacks however imaginary or bellowing keep consumptive. Hoardings of grain last longer peckings for land-days, each crop divide their own hand of it fatted, put to knife. Blood-saving behind them. Little ones earn their charnelhouse lie for each liver the name made gives wake. In a scar waning smudgy. Dense itself. As much harvest needs a horn claiming procession. It attempts escape toward eyeteeth following pineal organ—yet a release of ascending flesh, they become her perfumed blind.

dance obsidian veil them
around fill of breath
spilt vergences issue
release viridian gave
moor in from her
allure upon set ring
finger spindle over
await should zenith seen
pulse needing wake
duration itself mere if

Tip
     of a scale all stills in jeweled
incense their stop from granted
plummet, fastens up spiteless
thoughts in a spell her ministry
has instructed. On land, there treads
a coarse kindness—

         That temper-voice
       from my casing,
she keeps stake to obey this

             else.

eventual abundance ajars
as pierce heaviness its own
tempest leer alike a portent,
and when ceases nodding
does summon by clap against
its resting, a return over
the stand calling heaven's
attention filigree despite
spent reed in a guest shadow
or until some distantly
sea-yearning quotidian

hears alchemy rub cold
against the frail insides
a mothering for vanity
fine-tune the mutable
straw broom, would grasses
ever ancestor the stoneless
ruin destined to hear
the names hushed
upon its carnal walls,
forcing a leather riddle

to tapestry copper
boltings peeled from
crossed on wooden
beams, the flaying needles,
a glassy breadloaf broken
for fixtures mocking tiny,
gasping shells heated in
impossible drench up
towards the ceiling's dissent,
whereupon concocting
on tongue, a stirring relic
shares its poison

out from sturdy base, again
some ripe passion or the keep
afloat the hounded kneeling
by haystack arcane, emerging
then fastidious
with a mournful whim—evasive,
this incision—only they must let
celebrate the studies, they who sold
under candlelamp the gentle request
that partitions awaiting endless,
the given certitude left
unwashed to handle bent impressions,
subtlety its stubborn
ribcage language, nullifying bells
in their heave autumnal to spare
these last dampening fires
an attic rite
lusting for incursion

the finest springtime pillow,
a spare corset guessing her breasts
he groans for set knuckles, from drip
into blackened pan into the cauldron
peace, with never becoming a single,
forgetting twilit fault through being
let go covers reddened, shaming pages
past their touching, would his instill
cleanse marble scents of pushed-aside
doors, the heed attention intuitive
at regaling inertness of a stone's promise
to walk away on end,
enraged by a saving far past
this, them, itself

Nocturne breathes her aghast for her on the mantle's heat, a solemn gainsay left to be lacquered, not by his linseed oil but by the command of hearth in her unobstructed view, note by note, blushing out the sanguine bane she had torn from the roots beneath the house, all at once aflutter and shielding herself from its instrument, conceived without blessing, a patter left sensate to other obligations.

The careens their voices make shape silted detriments in the gathering.
Unfastened space they attend with no small remorse. Each pustule
and crack the waters moved over. Dens made assembly against wishes.
Quantity pooled together. Seeing themselves haggard befalls every
caprice mustered after circling lower depths, of watching skies not
touching precipices nor brushing spires lit in morning. Grace bereft
of occasional benefits. If saving recipient from mourning, their tribute
way: escape wails. Evocations disguised from cavern echo below their
feet. Ascent in likening to intended listener. Grottoes stilled ask trifles,
and finest waters draw arms folded. Rest for withal. The apprehensive
vessel their way above ground, tumbling dry winds into their mass of
voices. Survey stays these a place. They are forced to spit fresh stains.

Deluge lures sooner than animals ask passant. Bearing claimant teeth. Be that waterspout bends limbs of canine firmament without difficulty. The headlong crash into leathered beams lifting off roof-thatch stacked neat. Pacing indoors, he resolves lashing the frame onto splintered wooden stakes. A vicious rest otherwise will decide the sun shallowing under the horizon. Of serpentine year, he calls it, aslink round what age consumes its tail in own advance. Every measure of equal ground he stepped upon. Took furrow. Then not agreeable. Lost. Avulsions revealed bring about one early foal, it having been sprung from a lived-in filly tending farther pasture. Dishonest stares take toll of indentured sight: he follows the mother's thighs. Her ropish slather had carpeted—after the chalky-tinged sledding this hidden visitor meant. Belonging he waves his former pride away, and grass manifest in all portions natal.

Milling in thrice accompanies long slowing within her, the knuckles blandish at each demise, namely, an insect's crush on a thumb, but not leaving a print. All that they were, her hands: her utensils, her drawstrings, her spindlepoints. Made in weather for heated change she could encumber. She knows names as snowbreezes note their way through treetops lost in the windshake, a spot troubling for her to say aloud, asplay on her legs that dream in turning jewels on the mantlepiece, alone, unshaken. Slipping to him a pill yet unknown to them both.

Seawaves roll crashing a longer for heeding no more cries to help.
Surely those were from him in latter-day passages, he who brought his
own deaths. Immense plague and unrest. Masked pattern of following
crystal shatter. As eager faultlines those subunctuous trifles land, their
flesh absconds at a whim, now free from mooring. Scrolled broken
praises turn upwards. Rushed over by the very deep welcoming them.
Could this be another cold,

      they regress,

            accompanying our end eternally.

It does not enter their contemplations. Textures are interior lit with
faint scrutiny. Their terrible shelves set upon the need.

She is seen. And as seen, is faulted. The plate
off its movement but she loves her movement.
Bowing legs. Split of agility. Through water
origin names their running. A new moon shields
her temperament, a fixed gainsay sullying its proud
turn upward. There are those who can ride across
tainted surfaces if drawing care to a light kill.

Keeping tread on her evenhand, spheres
never ask why she leaves them there, never
hatch for her delight. Mere pebbles
having already nodded to sleep inside,
the sediment of spelling deathly a womb
which calls visitation upon their heads.

would that   base daze
worry her   enrapt in
a doorway   she pays
in stares   as rowings
save none   heed chop
and thrust   and speak

Chambers deigned her echo. Entrance drove
hollowed shafts below her. Finding water she
came to a bed of animals in their sloughing, fur
transparent to her lightening touch, a shade
wandering from what she knew as father, his
wetness and his blood. What could the strands find.
What did firmness demand but rest.

Tides dare caress themselves. Spill their albumen on the sands. Woe brings rocks for those to dwell under granted skies. Autumnals cease the instant they find grasses to their liking; and hiding in them, crafted hymns of cool shade. Their bellies no longer burnt. Their tongues no longer tasting saltwater. They leave themselves expanding in radiance over the inlet. Shells marble according to slew and slop of waving flow. They shed their scrim over alabaster spheres. Broken. They dent the surface upwards. Peek strong. White noses through lilies carried by stream. He spites at them,

       Leave your eggs on the banks. Feast instead on drizzle that rides infernal sightings,

       the refusal of this catch hardly staying his fury.

Soil-smooth they cricket onwards, dead on the weight, tussled over
quarter lengths. It is the right evening for apologia, some antlers prod
him, those honed in wooded columns where arcana grew. Blending
as sylvan creatures would, their affinities play husk and sortings. They
follow his perusal of the bankhead for shells but find only what has
split apart. Fruit missing rind. This group flails its captivity gone as
pressing by peculiar sounds. Then what cannot come from sky. Where
hovers his memory will recite years serpentine.

*Let sight within please this
terrain staring into instead, make those who rend at a touch,*

*it speaks,
for if drawn from waters, believe these shadows hence unbecoming.*

Indeed
his ripeness has not taken wait in vain. Fearsome these foundlings
scrounge, a blasted yea of them to greet. He strikes far too slender.
Pinning their bodies he crushes heads under spade-heel. Regarding each
spine takes much of his slack. He throws them upon limp water, and
into vague incarnation. Should crevasses stay them forsaken. He will
hope since he deems,

It is done,

sooner than it is.

Clairaudient illness dies one as a beast,

he would protest. A fever. Tiny swellings. Eyelidded heavy she falls silent over him. Fowl with red and black-crested mane often walk triumphantly enough. Sunlight pours upon this adoration. Cleansed by surrendered feathers, her dispatching blade lends no impurities to his quicken. Some blood keeps dry this ready pollution.

Meat, for helping. Did not the nearest
shave his pate when expiring? Not with
a son at bedside.
                    But where will my spirit go—
there,
        he plans, in books hidden. She fiddles
with matchsticks. Puts a roomless child to sleep
before him.

The deep, the dear, and regret. It could only be when turning to this
emerges with her finery. Notwithstanding bluster holding at her throat,
this evening drives into her unwelcomed and stays until satiated, well
beyond her means to host it.

It is good giving yourself staid,

a voice

within her countered, prickly, unassuming,

otherwise the bending would

slave you over yet.

But that was only gainsay milking a ruby from
her ear, lighting dance upon them until they melt. Then what pools
shimmered there, grinding into colors unseemly that they fail before
her eyes, and what bade the memory of color forth did not have the
luminous hue of earth but the fascination of its end, poor of the
discernable mark. Slovenly it reaches its hand for any help, and, finding
none, shears its facets, its angles and vertices, for any sanctuary.

Design for me
the manner of my passing,

              he asks her,

let yourself know what will happen
when my eyes look beyond
that farthest point this roof covers,
that no thatch can conceal
from its fatherly host:
sew my lifethreads together
with unbaited hooks
of curled iron and clamshell
once the mantle turns its head from me;
spill the scent from your legs at low tide
so I may avoid bin-death
in the ground columns;
draw my face
on honeycombs with your lip's heat
so its taste brings a final pleasure—
make all these a mask
for our child to gaze upon,

   while she paints
 brow cheeks mouth
with amber bird feathers.

Any grave holds its mistake long enough.
Without accompaniment to turn his into
silvered glass, it will not sleep while being
seen. Empty space where her kiss awaits
the lid. Gales pass over. The broken land
lays ahead for all feeding.

Consequence to all strategies against
the unknown may outlive her and the
child if it studied well. Kneeling before
the unsoiled curtain, touching its divide.
Whiteness another mask becoming. Her
perfection owns the familial minded.

Lullaby, until carving even
a mouth. Such the patience
on usual string. She teaches
the child breathing under its
chin, fingers and toes to curl
around the part hidden. Then
face of the mask must marry
itself to what was his chasm
in life. A spoonfed millstone.

Agony, though heaving, though the child ties her up. Loathe for caring in its listless mind. Giving in to the day tells the wind. Branches that held her there, bound her dissent in pearl-strings once extracted from a mare by him, left on slide below the pathway. The mind keeps her quietude into tea. The child not at all bitter. Holding himself up told these branches what was dearest to her still—nothing, least of all. What her mind cares for, the junipers loathe. Something sighed baits for her entirety, that his mask feels at home, up there, sitting on the mantle, and the child not so deceased yet.

This price for pity,
                she imagines:
constant illumes breaking against their distension; mill-torn wrappings
drawing the frayed edges into a supine hole to dangle the night watch;
unfastened yells to the attic shapes; opaque sighs on winter breaths;
cleaved ropes sent for the furnace; ink-spattered disavowals later
genuflected; tinderboxes emptied of sight; cornucopias of blood oranges,
black-seeded plums, molting peaches, apples sucked dry; bronzed teeth
in payment for lost tomes; dreary secrets of the uninitiated laity; foxcombs
and bonespears; the last mother-of-pearl weathervane; the urn of a child's
ashes; a scrap of vellum, a charcoal twig to fancy; diaries of cloudfilled
skies; splintered saltlicks; cured offal from unknown kill; an apothecary's
fingernail misplaced while scratching wooden beams for gold dust;
messianic treatises saved to prevent rapture; vials of quicksilver extracted
from a beast's womb; fossilized sugarcane with ants frozen within;

intrusions from the field's periphery dragging their splendor behind them; stagnant glint of an earring's turn from her dolloped lobe filled in stable agony between his fingers; goldleaf shed from a weeping ascent; a fatty liver ventured by the goose who lived twelve more years after its removal; a ball of smelted iron rods in an indeterminate puzzle; three velvet banners adorning the funeral parlor; a dress worn to second virginity; a tomb of magnesium sparing his body; totems ransacked from beyond the reach of glaciers; the destitute proclamation of utter forgiveness; weaving hornets in a carriage of pond reeds; pigments extracted from an unintentional suicide; shutters torn from false windows facing south; visages rebuilt from memory alone; a hermit's blessed sandals upon overcoming gout;

the daze of worms in blinding light; the prideful instinct of unaccustomed lunacies; candleholders blessed by impostors so their banishment may be revoked; lampshades condemned to their own dust; the boundless enthusiasm of conjoined twins; braided locks of sisters who fell in love with each other; a narcissus grown from the vine instead of the ground; a desultory map of ruinous lives radiating their magnetism; a sandal sleeping underwater; the handle of a rusted dagger blade left in the morning dew; whispers kept unattended in prison cages; deliriums returned by shelved desires waiting for their former master and mistress; vestments washed in bathwater salts; the senselessness of imminent ambrosia.

Equatorial line bounces her careless
in the seamscape. She bites the mask
on the lip and lets it bleed after a while.
The fluids feathering out their own
instinct near the thread-mark, his
husbandry, or the shale of his skull
giving space to another at the far end,
breaking her silence. Her bread.

Memorials obscure. Sending away the child hovers
in anticipation of fingers. Her figure among bales.
A stave milks the ground, fouling air for horses
reigned aside. More would come to pasture, clodding
earth into carbuncular form once again. That day will be
left paid on shame with barbs for tatters. Her raising struck
dumb by singularity, vanishing point of blindness into
a terrible well made a mote for the child's pain.
An underground chamber must be built from above. Brushing
aside sound below as water. It is soft claret snapping.
Amusing herself keeps this room lit longer with usage.

Hearing only themselves in lain gives the foals
a startle, expecting his tongue arriving in short,
slopped breaths, brushing aside their spill into
newer land. Hewing tools plentiful in abandon.
Trees their own harvest. For his burden stones
hold in lightened hands.

RESIDUALS

SEKAI

A GUST OF WIND had blown the orange off the pedestal.
I could stare.

With obeisance, the offering returns unless anything disturbs this night. The skin of fruit will drift hard and cold and soft and leave in leavings. Another may yet replace it or it still may not.

I perform obliteration to sit woodenly before a shape promising.

VOUCHSAFED

THESE HABITING SHOES, a book decrees, stand pat—*Politeness must transcend them with us*—outside an open double door of many fine woods, though the toes may head toward a vestibule where dirt should not be tracked; and few refinements help elude tracking, abstain from hesitation, if stepworn stairs in longshadow obligate the apoplectic guest to fumble pointed so his senses clear away service from the alcove, to play listening games for a prize in abhorrence, the hosts' welcome long ago returning astray, or his odd hand-written thing.

IN BECOMING NURSE

WHOSO BELIEVES NOT in ruin but renovation becomes
nurse; and in becoming nurse, not of being nurse, not of standing
anonymous and clean, not of being accustomed to the coming
ruination, the standing before moldering files of deceased and nearly
deceased and soon-to-nearly deceased that read blank, smudgy,
inescapable numbers, numbers attached to certain predilections to
weakness; and in becoming nurse there is hazard in a predilection
toward tidying lives beyond belief of becoming, those whoso sneak
in anonymously where none look where they should in weakening
rain; or should nurse stand with blank countenance unbecoming to
claim the ward, should nurse predict the number of beds, should nurse
reattach faces to them, a guess must be hazarded to renovate the one
who so lives beyond the drywall mold, nearly unreadable in the file of
anonymity, ceasing to believe in escape; and should the custom exist,
it exists; and should in becoming nurse one becomes not a number in
a tidy life but counting inescapable faces soon-to-nearly moldering in
their beliefs; and should there be hazard sneaking around unseen by
weakness; and wherefore then the ruin of the number of nurse stands
to cease with the number of smudgy beds escaping attention
or hazarding the escape, nurse soon believes.

IMMATERIAL

NEVER WASTEFUL: every pencil used to a nub-end. Let us proceed. A proposed debate on the floor about throwing away bite marks saved in the shaver until motion is tabled for recognizing distasteful habits give better grip.

THE PARIAH

I TOOK THE BOOK as far as I could with me, and let it go at the burning yard. It stayed there long after I was gone, I was told, along with the others left by those who followed me, who would not be gone. The fires burned night after night for those who would not be gone, could I believe they stayed as long as they did. If I did not want my book, then no one would have theirs. No one, they insisted. Night after night they took turns luring other books to the fire first followed by those who would have stayed after I was gone. Only the one who left told me this. Only the one who could not believe all the books were gone in the fires followed. Could I take only the one, I believed, then no one would follow me, and I let the one go who would not be gone. The fire burned night after night. No one would have theirs. No one, I insist.

A TRIPTYCH OF SAINTS

AGATHA OF CATANIA

Were slaves mended to this: matter found in shapeless destiny, toying with the agonies feet could rub against, for the host who bares forward on some privilege yet to be taken.

Until that day, remoteness must find these pincers a bane to your pleasure's touch, though unafraid of the healthy bent applied. To bestow oneself knotted, whole, dreary of never-ending noses scraping an ear, the last mirth I am to receive. You men speak benevolent without wine, when peeling your foreheads layer by layer as afterthought. A gifted body leaves none of its own reward for the keeper's kind, should He see it fit to shroud its manifest under crude sackcloth. Light the screams of approval, then. I am as generous as my own milk. I have given, and I have given. And from this I am truly filled with misgivings that serve not those who are served, who shall remain motionless on staircases. Consider the rise and the fall of such inconsequences that speed bodies to oftsame exhilaration.

Blend your flesh together. You all are enough for me.[1]

---

[1] Sebastiano del Piombo, *Martyrdom of Saint Agatha*, 1520, oil on panel. Public display in Pitti Palace, Florence, Italy (image taken from "Sex and Spirituality in Rome: Sebastiano del Piombo's *Martyrdom of Saint Agatha*," Jill Burke, *Art Bulletin*, September 2006, vol. 88, no. 3).

JOAN OF ARC

There are men with me who have already known the feint of my lips
against their heart, and secluded do find they are moving as they bait
with shoving lust above the pale in my eyes. They and I are formations.
Ear kisses ear in their orthodoxy, and we become memory intrusive.
The supple of an already wet cheek to spit upon the throng-stare. An
insect lands—twice, by my hand—to precede grace in subterfuge.
The comfort's friend, or the oval of his hand matching his face in
immolation (every shadow they will pounce upon). I abjure only to this
sacrament of flies. Of blood in the pan. In fairness has enough tear-spill
stained a letter of my supposal. And do shudder the lids, and throat in
shade and shale, there in a prison of lighted angles that seem to speak,
shorn of words. Rushing to me, servants of palaces corrupted by the
skull. I want to say that the earth, for them, is never safe. For I have
tied little robins made from my hair. I regret my signature into this
waiting stone. I am led into a basin.[2]

---

[2] *La passion de Jeanne d'Arc*, 1928. Dir. Carl Th. Dreyer. B/W. Silent.

Mother, it is not for hope that I try this remedy, nor the roped band around my waist. Do I dress for any man in his shallows? Does he take what will be brought back in full? You cannot guess. The air stifles. An answer lies in another woman's tomb I have sought, most holy—

and yet she refuses me. She is tired, she murmurs. Has attended many other than Him. Let her rest. Return again later. Leave. Now.

I obey. The dust will burn my feet, though to assure you are well. Preparations are barely made. A plate carried is an only pillow: where I am to succumb, if not an unbelieving marriage-bed of palm leaf, where sight entrusts me should it be plucked by the root. Should Restoration provide eyes of a far different hue than my choosing.[3]

---

[3] Traditional decorative statue. Public display in Saint Anthony of Padua Roman Catholic Church, Buffalo, New York.

UNREQUITED

IT MEANT EITHER not being fair to Bertie or us looking for her
shoe we had to find in the woods. It meant either not looking for the
shoe we had to find in the woods or racing Larry back home. It meant
either not racing him back home or downing him into muddy leaves
some more. It meant either not downing him into muddy leaves some
more or watching him damn us. It meant either not watching him
damn us or finding the rest of Bertie out there. It meant either not
finding the rest of her out there or stopping Larry's mouth up with
her fishnet stockings. It meant either not stopping his mouth up with
her fishnet stockings or him playing electric guitar with two-finger
chords. It meant either him not playing electric guitar with two-finger
chords or us setting ablaze the soft mountain that was Bertie's chemise
collection. It meant either not setting ablaze the soft mountain that was
Bertie's chemise collection or Larry making another heartbox out of a
boneyard August. It meant either him not making another heartbox
out of a boneyard August or us being to fair to Bertie.

NERVE

AN ADAMANT future of my fingernail came through on
my supervisor's bait. It took longer than expected. "Still," he
complimented, "a month is a month." Under the cutaneous layer
it had scraped to the quick smooth, its pearling predetermination
becoming shatterless—just like his. I bit at the nail determined, wore
it down until there was no difference between his Before and my After.
Hopefully I would hang by a thread.

SIAMESES

OUR I ESCAPES the movers. Sad, sad movers with that moving look while making moves. They carry the two-bit dirge away, ding it against the banister. They forget at the door their Chang and Eng manners. Bubblewrapped, the parlor now gives off a frontier transparency but far fewer throatings. The latter once included the I happily including us. All those previous occasions had not suitably embarrassed. Wantings of a criminal insertion remain. There are incidentals soon attached.

THE LUNG, THE FEATHER, THE TOOTH

NOT WAITING anymore, she parted his lips with her fingers
while he slept upstairs. He had said this before leaving with his book,
showing us with the pages what he meant. That was why she wasn't
here. That was why we then drew our last breath of him.

———

Sometimes waiting for her and knowing her wanted the same from
each of us. There were no measurements inside to satisfy pencil and
ruler. We went looking.

When we found a dead fox outside, we took a lung and left the
rest. The tailfeather off a gull. The incisor off something we couldn't say
or it wouldn't say since there was no speaking. The ocean lay calm, grass
took tall, wind settled for its own falter.

Our spoils required either dwelling upon or the utter lack thereof.

———

We made our beds downstairs as beds were thought to be made by her.
Tidy. Careful. In sleep she did visit us once. The sheets we were made
to clean every week with a bit of the ocean.

Beds made and unmade but ended with aimless hands in the dark.

On the floor arranged a circle. The lung, the feather, the tooth.
We grew unsure if there was ever a bed upstairs.

———

Glass for the windows broke. The door remained elsewhere. And the
chairs. He had never mentioned these while reading his book. Until the
sun set, we answered only by shaking our heads.

———

Where rain pattered off the roof kept little but a promise of the ocean.
The tooth not an incisor but a molar. The feather from another bird.
The lung fresh. Heavier for it.
    Her bed must be upstairs.
    Before morning the rain would often stop. We heard her coming
downstairs. We heard her as though she had always done this.
    "I was too soon," she said.
    She left us sleeping in our beds.

DEAREST

BE DEAREST he begs himself from the corner. Be called of him to lend those sweet bedsides now never offering her open eyes again, or her bed. Do not upset him, be on best behavior. Be careful of rope-burn. Do not pour his honey trail for ants tracing the stoop up towards her. No more of her when none mattered to him. As it is he languishes. Struggle he had sighted, the tiniest sort of genuflection thrown upon him, knees and feet upon him, across him. Blend violet and blue painted downstairs. Rusted-down covered. Find if his face was, too. Well, another day like today, then. Last message he asks. Keep the lessons crossed over a switch. Tongue and groove. Thin with turpentine. Preserve with linseed. Be on best behavior. Entertain. How two quarters sound rubbed together, copper dust at the edges. On the floor, or coppered floor. Decorate. Find a dustpan. Sweep the hallway away from around his bellows. Stay doorknobs latched with wire. Be dearest, watch from wooden chair, and he will breathe heaviest. Still at work polishing quartz. Not amethyst by her windowsill. He has moved them. Sunlight he says has moved them, not her spirit fingers. Be yesterday. Tie down her fingers. Do not block her doorway. Turn his hourglass on its head: it will seem like today now. Bit of oil is left. Feel better without him. Lights out he says. He sleeps off in the corner, sometimes he says with her. Was the right by and by for this happening. The changeling bedroom him and her kept feeding once sound, right again. They found. Suppose it was just him. Her trials furthest from him voicing them. Be speech. Spell out on his chalkboard. Show him. Have him read aloud over thunderclap or point to the dripping cascade instead. Ask permission before starting work. Correct each mistake his bowls capture. Paint a stairway, then walls, then the highest ceilings hands ever put to prove.

ACKNOWLEDGEMENTS

The flash fiction and prose poems in this collection were originally published in the following print and online journals, with much appreciation to all the editors of these:

5_Trope: "Drift"
alice blue review: "Sekai"
Bateau: "Paste"
Caketrain: "The Lung, The Feather, The Tooth"
Cardinal Sins: "The Alcoholic's Return"
Corium: "Keeping With"
The Corduroy Mtn.: "Trade"
Denver Quarterly: "A Triptych of Saints"
Dogplotz: "Drawstring"
Double Room: "Glossies"
Ekleksographia: "Roomiers"
elimae: "Immaterial," "Nerve," "Parcel Post Belgique," "Three Hundred
   Mile House"
Locus Novus: "Pure"
Mad Hatters' Review: "Dearest," "Fantasy of Trees in Silver"
NOON: "Nature," "Paper"
Quick Fiction: "Clean Dead Leaves," "The Mistress"
San Antonio Current: "Only If We Had Lived Here"

Snow Monkey: "Funny Little Bird"
Staccato: "Tender Spoils"
Starry Night Review: "Proust's Moustache"
Timber: "The Oblique Romantic" (online)
Tin Parachute Postcard Review: "The Bear Planet Edict"
Word Riot: "Afterbirthing," "Curio," "Vouchsafed"

Many thanks as well to Lyle Rosdahl for assembling and curating the *Postcard Fiction Collaborative* online where previous versions of these flash fictions first appeared: "Beets," "Business," "Dregs," "Echo," "A Few Areas of Note at Prospect Park," "In Becoming Nurse," "Instrument," "The Kitsch Giraffe," "Little Meat," "Middling," "Occasional," "The Other," "The Pariah," "Plurality," "Short Time with Hula Girl," "Siameses," "Some Baseball Stories," "Ten to One," "Unrequited," "Who Doesn't Enjoy a Good Sausage," "The Win."

"Only If We Had Lived Here" is a remix / revision of a text portion from Blake Butler's *Scorch Atlas* (2009) done for a Featherproof Books promotional contest, and was published with his kind permission.

Selections from "Autumnals" appeared previously and sometimes in different forms in *Caketrain, elimae, Foothill: a journal of poetry, Lonesome Fowl, Mud Luscious, Otoliths, Pinstripe Fedora,* and *Upstairs at Duroc.* A short sequence was also published as a chapbook, *The Sullen Pages,* by Little Red Leaves in 2013 for their Textile Series.

"Autumnals" is dedicated in loving memory of Dr. Marthe Reed for her gracious feedback and support of this work while chairing my dissertation at the University of Louisiana at Lafayette. Miss your laugh and everything, Marthe.

FORREST ROTH holds a Creative Writing Ph.D. from the University of Louisiana at Lafayette, and is a Visiting Assistant Professor of English at Marshall University in West Virginia. He is the author of a novella, *Line and Pause* (BlazeVOX, 2007), a prose poem chapbook, *The Sullen Pages* (Little Red Leaves, 2013), and a novel, *Gary Oldman Is A Building You Must Walk Through* (What Books, 2017). His short fiction has appeared in *NOON*, *Denver Quarterly*, *Juked*, *Columbia Journal*, *Trnsfr*, and other journals.

WHAT
BOOKS
PRESS

LOS ANGELES

2022

No One Dies in Palmyra Ohio
HENRY ELIZABETH CHRISTOPHER
NOVEL

Us Clumsy Gods
ASH GOOD
POEMS

Skeletal Lights From Afar
FORREST ROTH
FLASH FICTION/PROSE POEMS

That Blue Trickster Time
AMY UYEMATSU
POEMS

2021

Pyre
MAUREEN ALSOP
POEMS

What Falls Away is Always
HAAKE & WRONSKY, EDITORS
ESSAYS

The Eight Mile Suspended Carnival
REBECCA KUDER
NOVEL

Game
M.L. WILLIAMS
POEMS

2020

No, Don't
ELENA KARINA BYRNE
POEMS

One Strange Country
STELLA HAYES
POEMS

*Remembering Dismembrance:
A Critical Compendium*
DANIEL TAKESHI KRAUSE
NOVEL

Keeping Tahoe Blue
ANDREW TONKAVICH
STORIES

2019

Time Crunch
CATHY COLMAN
POEMS

Whole Night Through
L.I. HENLEY
POEMS

Echo Under Story
KATHERINE SILVER
NOVEL

Decoding Sparrows
MARIANO ZARO
POEMS

2018

Interrupted by the Sea
PAUL LIEBER
POEMS

The Headwaters of Nirvana
BILL MOHR
POEMS

2017

*Gary Oldman Is a Building
You Must Walk Through*
FORREST ROTH
NOVEL

Rhombus and Oval
JESSICA SEQUEIRA
STORIES

Imperfect Pastorals
GAIL WRONSKY
POEMS

2016

The Mysterious Islands
A.W. DEANNUNTIS
STORIES

The "She" Series: A Venice Correspondence
HOLADAY MASON & SARAH MACLAY
POEMS

Mirage Industries
CAROLIE PARKER
POEMS

2015

*The Balloon Containing the Water
Containing the Narrative Begins Leaking*
RICH IVES
STORIES

The Shortest Farewells Are the Best
CHUCK ROSENTHAL & GAIL WRONSKY
LITERARY COLLAGE/PROSE POEMS

2014

It Looks Worse Than I Am
LAURIE BLAUNER
POEMS

They Become Her
REBBECCA BROWN
NOVEL

*The Final Death of Rock-and-Roll
& Other Stories*
A.W. DEANNUNTIS
STORIES

Perfecta
PATTY SEYBURN
POEMS

2013

Brittle Star
ROD VAL MOORE
NOVEL

Sex Libris
JUDITH TAYLOR
POEMS

Start With A Small Guitar
LYNNE THOMPSON
POEMS

Tomorrow You'll Be One of Us
WRONSKY, ROSENTHAL, GRONK
ART/LITERARY COLLAGE/POEMS

2012

The Mermaid at the Americana Arms Motel
A.W. DEANNUNTIS
NOVEL

The Time of Quarantine
KATHARINE HAAKE
NOVEL

Frottage & Even As We Speak
MONA HOUGHTON
NOVELLAS

*West of Eden:
A Life in 21ˢᵗ Century Los Angeles*
CHUCK ROSENTHAL
MAGIC JOURNALISM

2010

Master Siger's Dream
A.W. DEANNUNTIS
NOVEL

Other Countries
RAMÓN GARCÍA
POEMS

A Giant Claw
GRONK
ART
ESSAY BY GAIL WRONSKY
SPANISH TRANSLATION
BY ALICIA PARTNOY

Coyote O'Donohughe's History of Texas
CHUCK ROSENTHAL
NOVEL

So Quick Bright Things
GAIL WRONSKY
POEMS
BILINGUAL, SPANISH TRANSLATION
BY ALICIA PARTNOY

2009

Bling & Fringe (The L.A. Poems)
MOLLY BENDALL & GAIL WRONSKY
POEMS

April, May, and So On
FRANÇOIS CAMOIN
STORIES

One of Those Russian Novels
KEVIN CANTWELL
POEMS

*The Origin of Stars
& Other Stories*
KATHARINE HAAKE
STORIES

Lizard Dream
KAREN KEVORKIAN
POEMS

*Are We Not There Yet? Travels in
Nepal, North India, and Bhutan*
CHUCK ROSENTHAL
MAGIC JOURNALISM

As a small, independent press, we urge our readers to support independent booksellers. This is easily done on our website by purchasing our books either through Indiebound or from BookShop.

WHATBOOKSPRESS.COM

www.ingramcontent.com/pod-product-compliance
Lightning Source LLC
Chambersburg PA
CBHW030939210726
48290CB00007B/2246